DEAD MAN'S HAND
and
THE DEVIL'S HANGMAN

by

L. Jackson and V. Britton

L. Jackson and V. Britton

1-14-06

WHISKEY CREEK PRESS
www.whiskeycreekpress.com

Published by
WHISKEY CREEK PRESS

Whiskey Creek Press
PO Box 51052
Casper, WY 82605-1052
www.whiskeycreekpress.com

Copyright © 2004 by *L. Jackson and V. Britton*

ISBN 1-59374-232-0

Credits
Cover Artist: Ed Britton
Editor: Ximena Carter

Printed in the United States of America

Dedication

~~To Gary Britton and Diaz Jackson, two real cowboys. With special thanks to Ed Britton for the cover.~~

DEAD MAN'S HAND

"Wild Bill" Hickok

"Wild Bill" Hickok, wild no lie,
Stagecoach driver and Union spy.
As fearless a man as the West has seen,
Fit to be Marshal of Abilene.

Restless traveler, couldn't keep still,
Toured the land with "Buffalo Bill."
In Deadwood, South Dakota, he met his downfall,
Shot in the back by Jack McCall.

"A U.S. Marshall must always be on guard,"
That was the warning in every card.
Two black eights, aces a pair,
Dead Man's Hand--better beware.

No one grieved for Bill like Calamity Jane,
Yet in the hearts of many his memory did remain.
To this day each Westerner will,
Speak a word of praise for old "Wild Bill."

"Wild Bill" Hickok, wild, no lie,
Stagecoach driver and Union spy.
As fearless a man as the West has seen,
Fit to be Marshal of Abilene.

L. Jackson

Dead Man's Hand

Modern Day Wyoming:

Jack Handley's dark eyes lifted from the cards and skimmed the four men around the poker table. A crew capable of giving even a dead man the shivers, he thought.

Directly across from him, the twins, Clint and Claude Baker, assumed the exact same expression, one able to stop a mafia godfather dead in his tracks. Their lean faces remained impassive as they regarded Jack with eerie patience.

Jack shifted the two fours to the left and said, "Three."

Jack's gaze raised to the dealer, to Dusty Pontier, whose desert camouflage jacket blended with his sandy colored hair and skin. He had eyed Dusty Pontier earlier as he had fanned the cards, gathered, and shuffled them in one deft motion. Now Jack noted the speed of his lean, quick fingers as he skimmed off the cards, his voice much slower than his movements as he counted, "One, two, three."

A two of clubs, a five of diamonds, and a seven of spades—identical to the hands he had gotten all afternoon. He looked into Dusty's pale eyes—the luck of the draw or a professional cheat?

When it came Jack's turn again, he knew his hesitation had given him away—no use attempting a bluff. "Too rich for me," he said, tossing down his cards.

The old man beside Jack chuckled, as he did from time to time. If Jack liked any of them, it would be Mort Jenkins, a hanger-on from the old West. His long, gray mustache matched the color of his twinkling eyes, which now glowed good-naturedly from their background of leathery, sun-darkened skin. Jack returned Mort's smile, thinking as he did that more often than not the ones he chose to trust proved to be the worst of the lot.

Not in this case, though. The worst of this lot, without question, throne and crown, went to Dusty Pontier. Jack had met Dusty during his short stay in the Laramie jail. Once Dusty had found out that Jack possessed ample cash, he had been quick to invite him to this high-stakes poker game, held at the famous Lucky Draw Hotel, tucked away in the Snowy Range Mountains west of Laramie.

Dusty's full attention turned to the twins, calculating eyes, narrowed and peering as if from out of the bars of death-house prison cells. The brothers, identical in features and slicked-back, black hair, looked at one another, some unspoken message passing between them. Jack thought for a minute they had made a silent agreement to fold. Instead Clint slowly slid bills to the center of the table, saying, "I'll meet and raise four hundred." Claude lost no time following his lead.

The old man, Mort, gave another chuckle and sent his cash forward.

Suspense mounted. Even though Jack himself had opted out, he felt as if his hands were gripping the fuse of a bomb. He slid back his chair, ran a hand across the tight muscles of his neck. He could be halfway home by now. That's where he should have headed, back to Phoenix to start looking for a job, instead of joining this group of professional gamblers. These tension-charged games, his second sense warned, were certain to end in some colossal disaster.

* * * *

Once up in his room Jack counted his losses. He drew in his breath. He had lost over three thousand dollars. Dusty Pontier, the big winner, had likely walked away with around ten grand. Jack wasn't prepared for another day like this one.

He stood at the upstairs window and gazed at the dark shadow of mountains, then at the trail of twisting road that wound its way into Laramie. He couldn't get the faces of the four poker players out of his mind—a psycho biker, twin gangsters who looked like Chicago hit men, a rough and ready cowboy with a lifetime's experience at outwitting and out-maneuvering his opponents—all extremely dangerous men.

Jack should have known better than to take Dusty Pontier, who he had met at the Laramie detention center, up on any kind of invitation. Pontier had been on his way to Sturgis, South Dakota, to meet up with some pals, a trail of enemies from a rival biker gang following close behind. A rowdy fight at a Laramie bar had earned him a stay in the local jail.

Jack didn't know why Dusty Pontier had sorted him out to befriend. Jack had thought at first that the biker had merely felt sorry him, for in lock-up Jack was far out of his usual element. Probably, instead, it had been Jack's mention of a recent cash settlement for a job-related insurance claim that had drawn Pontier's interest. Whatever the reason, Pontier had gone out of his way to run interference between him and the town ruffians. Jack owed him one, which is probably why he had agreed to join this poker game, which Dusty Pontier had claimed, would be cancelled if he couldn't come up with another player.

"The Baker twins are superstitious as well as stupid," Pontier had said. "They always refuse to play unless there's five at the table."

Jack thought of the hateful eyes of the twins as they had glared at the biker as he had stuffed his winnings into the leather pouch he wore over one shoulder. Even the old man's envious eyes had burned into the back of Pontier's fatigue jacket as he had left the room. Jack was almost glad he hadn't won, almost relieved his pockets were empty instead of filled with money previously owned by those three.

His fingers on the ledge had grown stiff and cold. Jack turned away from the window gripped by a sudden urgency to get away—to set off right now in the dead of night. But in the end his rational side overruled him. His leaving could wait until morning.

At the first light of dawn, Jack slung his personal effects into his duffle and headed down the curving steps into the vast lobby. The same attractive, auburn-haired woman who had checked him into the hotel yesterday looked up from her post behind the desk. "You're not leaving?" She hesitated as if his staying loomed as very important to her. "I thought you planned to stay at least until the weekend."

Jack's gaze rose from the nametag on the oak desk, Liane Vale, to the lovely owner of the Lucky Draw Hotel. The sight of her made him wish he were checking in again instead of leaving.

"I've had a change of plans," he said.

Liane fit in with the elegant surroundings, with beaded lamps and dark mirrors, an old-fashioned girl with wide, amber eyes and soft reddish-brown curls that hung loose this morning past her shoulders. For a moment he remained, aware of the deep sadness that had crept into her eyes, sadness that matched his own. Emptiness that Darla had caused.

He had been engaged to Darla, and after his injury at work had left Arizona to pay her a surprise visit. He had been the one surprised, had found her in bed with another man, the reason for his being thrown into the slammer. He had gone half out of his mind; Darla's lover had gotten a broken jaw and Jack had gotten thirty days. He felt the mighty impact again, the crumbling of his first, sweet love, the ruination of all the plans he had put together for her.

"I take it yesterday's game didn't go well for you," Liane was saying.

He smiled and tried to sound as if he didn't really care. "Up one day, down the next."

"So you're not staying for another round?"

For a moment he felt the tugging of temptation, then reminded himself that he had secured the insurance money, designated for Darla and him, back in a safety deposit box in Phoenix. After yesterday's losses, his checking account held only enough money for the trip home.

He stopped at the entrance. "I might be back this way...some day."

His leaving seemed to add to that look of burden, which she brushed aside with a forced smile. "Don't rush off without breakfast," she said quickly. "It's included in the bill."

Young and alone and lost—did she always look that way?

"I would even be free to join you," Liane encouraged.

That was more temptation than he could resist. Jack returned and set the duffel beside the desk. He followed Liane into a huge dining room, opulent in the subdued light. When he had eaten here at noon yesterday, the wine-colored, velvet drapes across the huge windows had been open to the beautiful view of the mountains.

Jack could see their images in one of the full-length mirrors. He liked the way they looked together. He towered above her, craggy features appearing tough and capable—and Liane, this woman could never look any way but gorgeous.

Liane led him to a small table near the fireplace where leaping flames crackled pleasantly. The smell of frying bacon wafted from the kitchen reminding him that he had missed last night's evening meal.

"We'll take two full breakfasts," Liane said to the waitress before she seated herself across from him. A crystal chandelier, dimly lit, enhanced her high cheekbones, her full lips.

"What brings you to Wyoming?" she asked.

He told her about the ruination of his romance. Liane listened, large eyes compassionate and that boosted his spirits. He thought suddenly, the wreck of his romance didn't have to mean the wreck of his life.

Jack looked at her, then glanced quickly away, warning himself against falling into the old rebound scene. Anyway, why did he think a perfect woman like Liane would be interested in someone like him—a loser who had nothing going for him but a generous insurance settlement?

Jack, groping for conversation that would drown out his self-pitying thoughts, indicated the huge picture hanging above the fireplace. "'Wild Bill' Hickok's last game," he said aloud.

For a moment he studied the flowing hair, the broad shoulders of the famous gunslinger, who was seated with his back to the door moments before his death. Jack McCall lurked in the shadow of the doorway, ready to fire that fatal shot. Somehow, the painting made him uneasy.

He spoke sardonically, "I thought this was supposed to be the Lucky Draw Hotel."

"Grandfather loved that painting," Liane said softly. She sipped coffee, looking at him across the fragile rim of china cup. "He won this hotel in a poker game, which is the reason for its name."

"Doesn't sound like Wild Bill's luck," Jack returned.

"But it was the other player's luck. You see." She leaned forward. "The man Grandfather played against ended up with the exact same cards that 'Wild Bill' Hickok was dealt in his final game. Grandfather beat him with a full house." Her gentle laughter rippled through the quietness of the room. "Grandfather reveled over that fact all of his life. He even hired a man from Cody to paint this picture for him. The whole episode has become a believe-it-or-not legend treasured by local card-players."

"I'm not much of a gambler," Jack said, as the waitress brought platters of bacon, eggs, and fluffy pancakes. "I took it up out of boredom when I was in the army and haven't played much since."

"I'm not either, but this event did set me up for life. My husband, Robert, loved the hotel and encouraged me to continue sponsoring poker games."

What had happened to Robert? He wanted to ask, but didn't.

"See that photograph near the window? That's Robert standing behind Grandfather's chair. It was taken right before Grandfather's final illness."

Jack appraised the older man first, a fine gentleman with snow-white hair, whose features put him in mind of Liane's. Then he studied the young man, handsome and smiling.

The pain crept back into Liane's large, amber eyes. "Robert died in a car accident last May. Over a year now. But it still seems just like yesterday."

Jack wanted to reach across the table and grip her hand, to say, "I'm sorry," but he didn't. He just watched her, feeling again a mingling of their sorrow.

Finally realizing he had lingered over breakfast as long as he could, he pushed back his chair. "Time to go," he said.

Liane made no move. "Do you really have to leave?"

"Since yesterday's losses, I find I can't afford to stay any longer." He explained to her about the state of his inaccessible funds.

Liane laughed breezily. "If that's all, I'll take a note from you. You can send me a check later when you get back to Phoenix."

Liane's offer battered like ocean waves against his wall of resistance. If he stayed on, maybe he could win back what he had lost; maybe he would win even more and become a big man in her eyes—like her grandfather, like Robert Vale. Jack didn't want to stay because of the poker game; he wanted to stay here because of her.

Caution stopped him from accepting. Liane had no reason to be taking risks like this. Could this be part of a set-up, a plot that might well involve them all—the twins, Mort Jenkins, Dusty Pontier, and this woman? Did they purposefully seek out some sucker, some hapless victim with plenty of cash? Jack got a quick vision of all of them laughing together as they divided their ill-gotten gains.

"If I did that, I'd just add loss to loss. I'd lose today's game, be suckered into another one, and then lose that. No, I'd better be going."

"You don't have to play. Didn't you hear the weather report? It's going to storm. At least stay another day," Liane encouraged. "Your note would be good for that, too."

"Notes aren't good security," he said, as if their roles were reversed.

"What if I took your money and ran out?"

"I know who can be trusted and who can't," she replied.

"Thanks, but no." Jack got to his feet, not turning back to her until he reached the doorway. Looking back was his downfall.

"As far as I can tell, you don't have any special reason to

return to Arizona. Once you get back there, you'll just be looking for a job. Why don't you hang around here? There's lots of work around Laramie."

Jack's heart thudded against his chest. He had been wrong about her. She wasn't in on any plot to trick him into staying and losing the rest of his cash; she really liked him. The attraction Jack felt for her, she, too, must feel. And what kind of a man could walk out on that?

"As I told you, my money supply is in a bank in Phoenix."

"As I told you," Liane replied, "I'll take an IOU for any reasonable amount."

Jack wanted to look away, but he felt powerless to do so. He sighed inwardly. If this were a trap, it had sprung, and he was caught. Still, he asked, "Why would you be willing to do that for a perfect stranger?"

Liane's lips became touched again with one of her slow, alluring smiles. She watched him closely, her amber eyes veiled in the dim light. "My whole life, this hotel, I inherited from my grandfather. But I sometimes think I may have inherited much more—perhaps just a little of Grandfather's gambling blood."

* * * *

Mort Jenkins sat alone in the poker room idly shuffling cards. His shaggy, gray head inclined toward the radio, as if he didn't want to miss a word of the advice given to the lovelorn. Like yesterday, he wore jeans and a faded, flannel shirt, sleeves rolled, revealing sturdy arms accustomed to hard work.

"Where is everyone?" Jack asked. "I thought the game was scheduled for ten."

Mort answered with a short laugh. "Anxious to lose your money, are you?"

"I wasn't thinking of losing."

"You'd better be." Mort's gnarled hands stopped their practiced motion. "I didn't win a single game yesterday. And that ain't natural." The usual sparkle in his eyes had become a cold glitter. "If anyone asked me, I'd say a whole lot of cheating was going on."

"I don't know," Jack returned quickly. "Pontier's game is poker and he's very skilled at it."

Mort seemed not to hear him. "The twins and I talked last night. They're convinced he pulled some fast-finger deals."

Talk like this, true or not, would start a blaze sure to end in smoke and ashes. Jack, preparing to make another attempt to counteract Mort's suspicions, was stopped by the entrance of the Baker twins.

Claude, who looked the meeker of the two, if not the wiser, remained by the door. Clint strode on into the room. "Can't you get some country music instead of that hogwash?" he asked, casting an irritable glance toward the radio.

Mort began to shuffle the cards again. "It's not hogwash. I like it."

Clint changed his voice to a shrill pitch in mimic of the program. "My word, my husband is cheating on me again. What on earth shall I do?"

Mort's motion with the cards ceased. "You don't have one sign of a heart, do you, Baker? You just don't care a fig about other people's problems."

Clint pulled out a chair. "Got enough of my own."

Claude, still near the door, laughed appreciatively. Then he strolled in and took a seat beside his brother, saying, "So, where's that good ole' cheat, Pontier? Still counting our money?"

Mort leaned forward conspiratorially. "Here's what we're going to do today, boys. We'll all work together. Give Pontier a taste of his own medicine."

The twins exchanged glances. Jack immediately rose to his feet. "That's not the way I play," he said. "You can count me out."

Jack started toward the door, Mort's laughter following after him. "Just joking, Jack," he drawled. "Can't get from day to day without a joke or two, now can we?"

The twins guffawed in unison. Jack, feeling foolish, reluctantly retraced his steps back to the table and again took a seat beside Mort. The brothers began talking to one another about their plans to go from here to Vegas.

"Where do you go next?" Jack asked Mort.

"I lost my son about a year ago—he was all I had. Since I had sold my ranch near Medicine Bow, I took to drifting."

"What made you return to Wyoming?"

"A man gets tired of tumble-weeding around," Mort said, sounding like a character from a Louis L'Amour western. "So I ended up at the Lucky Draw Hotel, and what do you know, I like it. Liane let me a permanent room, and I make enough playing cards to pay for it. Not that I don't have some back-up cash, too. What about you, boy? You going to stick around here?"

"Probably not."

Mort chuckled. "Most men would like being in your shoes. Liane's a bit smitten with you, in case you don't know it."

Jack, not wanting to go there, switched the track. "Did you ever meet her husband, Robert?"

"Sure, we played poker at Swenson's Bar from time to time. Heard he got dead drunk one night and crashed on the high road just east of here. But whatever happened to him, that pretty little girl has grieved long enough. Being alone is a tough game and don't I know it."

He shuffled cards again, delaying a long time before he

spoke. "Loss can make a person sort of crazy," he said.

Mort's statement, which hung tensely in the air, seemed to bear direct reference to Liane. Mort must possess some information concerning her reaction to Robert Vale's accident, some rash deed or deeds prompted by her grief. A sense of alarm washed over Jack as he wondered: *just how rash were they?*

The brothers had lost interest in their travel plans. Clint said, "Pontier knows we start right on time. He's already forty-five minutes late."

"Where the hell is he?" Claude demanded.

"Let's start without him," Jack said.

The brothers both shifted in their chairs and gaped at him as if he had suggested that they commit suicide.

"They won't play unless there's five at a table," Mort spoke up affably.

"Then I'll go see where he is," Jack replied, glad enough to be exiting the room.

Just outside the door Jack came face to face with Liane. His unexpected appearance caused her to flush, to awkwardly rebalance the tray of drinks she carried. As Liane gazed at him, an animation he hadn't noticed there before lit her amber eyes. Instead of being glad over her schoolgirl reaction to his presence, Mort's words began drumming through his head, "Loss makes people a little crazy."

He overran these thoughts with a question toned much louder than he had intended, "Have you seen Dusty Pontier?"

"I saw him leave early this morning. In fact, I warned him about the washouts in the roads after a hard rain."

"Where was he going? Do you know?"

"He probably went into Laramie."

"He might have run into some trouble with his bike," Jack said. "I think I'll take a drive out that way and see if I can find him."

Liane's voice drifted after him as he moved toward the hotel entrance. "When you get to that fork in the road," she said, "most people take the low road to the left. But Dusty wouldn't. He'd take the high road, a short-cut to town that saves about four miles."

* * * *

Jack headed toward his truck, drenched in seconds by the pelting rain.

When Jack reached the fork in the road, he made a sharp left turn onto a path he wouldn't have taken had it not been for Liane's instructions. Sheets of rain across the mountainside hampered his visibility. From time to time he was forced to stop the truck, emerge, and survey the deep gorges below.

On one such time, he looked back toward the high, stone turret of the Lucky Draw Hotel and noted with alarm that a person stood out on the widow's walk. Rain obscured the form, hand lifted to shield eyes from the rain, like the statue of some Indian scout. Before Jack had fully swung around, the vision vanished, making him wonder if it had actually been there at all or was merely an illusion of clouds and moisture.

With growing reservations Jack's attention returned to the truck trying to control the skidding tires as he inched his way up the muddy incline. Once the road leveled off, he managed to gain speed, attempting to steer around the puddles that had settled into deeply eroded ruts.

Just ahead the narrow trail of road curved horseshoe style around a steep cliff. Jack's hands tightened around the wheel. A premonition of what he would find lurked beneath the level of his conscious thoughts—a storm, a wreck. Like Mort Jenkins, Jack had no doubt that Pontier had cheated them all yesterday. But the devil take the money. Jack just wanted to find Dusty safe and sound.

As he rounded the sharp curve, from far below he caught a glint of silver. Jack stopped the car, jumped out, and peered over the embankment. Dread caused his throat to constrict as he hurried, feet sliding, down into the gully toward the grotesque tangle of bike.

When he reached it, he stopped, rain pelting his face as he skimmed boulders and foliage for Pontier. His gaze locked on Pontier's camouflage jacket, wet and glistening, blending with rock, leaves, and mud. He didn't need to step closer to tell that he had arrived too late.

Blood that had gushed from his wounds mingled with the stream of water beneath him. Jack started to reach out for him, to make sure he was dead, but his hands lost their ability to carry out his command. A hole from a high-powered bullet had pierced Pontier's helmet. Another one had caught him at the base of his neck and a third in the center of his back.

Without thinking, ruled by horror instead of judgment, Jack turned Pontier around. He didn't need to check his pulse. Pale, dilated eyes stared straight up.

"Good God!"

Jack felt as if he had lost a friend, even though he knew that wasn't true. Pontier had manipulated the game from the beginning, had cheated him out of even more than he had the others. As Jack thought of just how much he had lost, realization poured over him. Jack had served thirty days for the well-deserved beating of Darla's lover. The sheriff would be sure to believe that Jack himself had shot Pontier. He would never be able to explain how he had miraculously driven through a blinding downpour directly to where Pontier lay dead. Not a miracle at all, Jack thought, drawing back, hands shaking. Liane had directed him to this very spot.

Jack rubbed his cold fingers through his wet hair and across his face. The action seemed to restore him. Liane couldn't have any part in this. He should be blaming Mort Jenkins, not Liane. After all, Mort had enraged Clint and Claude Baker, goading them with Pontier's cheating until the twins, being who they were, had reaped vengeance.

Jack recalled how at the Laramie jail Pontier had laughed curtly and said, "You have to watch your back with those Baker twins. They play only one game: The Baker's win. They have a reputation for following the lucky ones from bars and casinos and rolling them for their winnings."

Again without thinking, Jack reached under the fatigue jacket and opened the bag Pontier wore belted under his shoulder. Empty. Pontier had been robbed of yesterday's winnings and no telling how much more!

Unable to believe it, Jack ran his hand inside the leather pouch, finding what the killer or killers must have left—a single card. Droplets of water fell across it causing it to glisten, wet and evil—the ace of clubs.

* * * *

On the phone Jack had given full account of what had taken place to the sheriff, explaining briefly about the poker game and the money, leaving out nothing, not even about finding the card. Then he went up to his room. He stood under the hot shower until he ceased shaking, quickly toweled off, dressed, and came back down the stairs. Mort and the twins stood beside the sheriff, who had been asking Liane questions.

Liane looked relieved to see Jack. "This is our sheriff, Morgan Spence," she told him.

"We've met," Spence said shortly. Spence, a burly man of about fifty, looked as if he had never smiled, thick lips frozen in a downward droop. He turned back to Liane. "How many people are registered at the hotel?"

"Seventeen."

"Of course I will want to talk to all of them."

"I can supply you with their names and permanent addresses. Some of them have checked out already. This tragedy will be sure to ruin my business."

She spoke matter-of-factly, totally without defeat or self-pity. Jack liked that; he had always admired strong, independent women.

"You were the last person to talk to Pontier. You say you had no idea where he was headed." The sheriff paused. "You say carrying large amounts of cash never bothered him. He didn't ask that the hotel secure his winnings."

"That's right."

The sheriff, remaining stern and focused, waited for Jack to reach the bottom step. "How much did you lose in yesterday's game?"

Clint Baker answered for him. "Everyone lost about the same, two or three thousand."

"Can you be more explicit? Exactly how much did you lose?"

"Three thousand," Jack said.

"I lost my shirt, too. Two-fifty," Mort put in.

"How about you, Mr. Baker?"

Clint and Claude exchanged glances, then Clint gestured to Claude. "He lost two-fifty. I lost two. That's chicken feed for high rollers," he said.

"And that's what you are?" Spence asked, looking them over, lips drawing more than ever downward. He turned to Mort. "Are you a professional gambler, too?"

Mort chuckled. "I wouldn't say that. Since I've moved into this hotel, going on three months now, I play a little. That's all."

"I've searched Pontier's room, and there wasn't a penny in it." The sheriff's full attention shifted back to Jack, thinking, without doubt, of the fight that had landed him in jail. Jack could tell by the narrowing of his eyes that Spence had already tagged him worthless, violent, which, in fact, he wasn't. In truth, Jack had always avoided fights. Darla's beau, one of Laramie's big-shot citizens, married, to boot, could blame himself for the beating he got, the way he had turned on Darla, insulted her, tried to blame her for his own damnable behavior.

"So you went out and found Dusty Pontier. They tell me you weren't gone long, not more than twenty minutes."

"That's right," Jack said, knowing he had made what might be a fatal error in turning Pontier's body around, in checking to see if he had been robbed, leaving his own fingerprints in the packet where Pontier had kept his winnings.

"In this storm, how were you able to find him so quickly?"

"I was looking for places where his bike might have spun out of control on some curve. Like I told you on the phone, when I found him, I turned him over to see if he was alive."

"What made you look in the leather pouch?"

"To see if he had been robbed."

Mort stepped protectively between Jack and the sheriff. "You're on the wrong track thinking Jack had anything to do with this. Or any of us at this hotel, for that matter, Dusty told me himself that those three bikers he had fought at Swenson's Bar were still after him. I reckon they finally caught up with him."

"Why were they looking for him? Do you know?"

"I wouldn't think you'd have to ask. Cards. Cheating. That's why they left that tell-tale ace."

* * * *

The threatening darkness from outside had encroached into Jack's room, hovering over him, streaking his every thought with shades of dismal gray. This very minute the sheriff would be attempting to put together a case against him, and he wasn't going to stand by and let that happen. By necessity he would try his hand at tracking those bikers that had been trailing Pontier.

Jack waited until the rain had slackened, then took the long route into Laramie. He stopped at Swenson's Bar on the outskirts of town. Inside, a group of old men sat around a swaying round table playing dominoes. A slight, middle-aged man with blonde hair that hung limply around his lean, sardonic face busied himself behind the bar. Jack perched on the stool.

The bartender acknowledged Jack's presence without looking around. "What's your poison?"

"Nothing, now."

The small man turned around slowly. "You just came in here to look at me? I'm flattered."

Jack smiled. "Are you the owner?"

"I am, but remember this: Swenson sees nothing, hears nothing, repeats nothing."

"I'm not here to cause trouble for anyone. I just need some information about Dusty Pontier."

Swenson held up his hands. "I told all the details of that battle to the sheriff. Go ask him. That's all I know."

"I'm a friend of Dusty's," Jack said. "I need to find out just what happened that night. Who caused the fight?"

"Those three, lunatic bikers, that's who. They started a verbal battle with Dusty the minute they came in. Dusty couldn't ignore them and things went from bad to worse. The way it ended, Dusty broke a bottle and cut one of them up good. Dusty ended up in jail and that pack of hoodlums walked." He added indignantly, drying his hands on a once-white apron. "I asked the sheriff why that was; didn't seem right to me. He said you can say anything you want to, but you can't lay a hand on another person, no matter what."

"Have you seen those three bikers since?"

"Nope. I understand they went on to Sturgis."

"It's possible that they found Dusty before they left." Jack continued, telling the bartender just how Dusty Pontier had died.

Swenson paled and turned away. "I've known Dusty for years." His voice had grown low and hollow. "Dusty was rowdy, but deep down he was a good Joe."

Silence fell, as dreary as the battered bar and the faded walls. At last Swenson began taking glasses from a wire basket and arranging them on the shelves above the bar counter. "He sure didn't deserve to end up like that."

"What do you know about Mort Jenkins? Does he ever come in here?"

"Of course." Swenson looked around suspiciously. "But don't be thinking he'd have anything to do with shooting Dusty."

"I've been playing cards with him; just mentioned him out of curiosity."

"Poor Mort, first he lost his wife, then about a year ago, his son. I knew the boy, too. Mort Jr.," Swenson said, "the spittin' image of Mort, but not nearly so," he tapped his temple, "shrewd. They lived on a ranch up around Medicine Bow. Junior used to wander in from time to time looking for a poker game."

"What happened to him? I wondered, but I didn't want to ask Mort."

"Some freak hunting accident. Squelched some big plans. The old man had just sold his ranch and the two of them were going to head off for California. His boy's death crushed him good."

"Mort Jr. was a friend of Robert Vale's, wasn't he?" Jack inquired.

"Liane's husband? Yeah, if you could believe that man had any friends." He wiped his hands again, saying, "Never liked that one. He was always on the lookout for someone to roll."

"He died in a wreck, didn't he?"

"Gasoline tank caught fire. He was burned to a crisp. Long before that I had flat told him I didn't want him playing poker at my bar. Cheating people, that's what he was good at, and I never am one to court trouble."

"So he moved his poker playing to the hotel," Jack said.

"And down the street to other bars in town. He was a real gambler—got in any game he could find. But gambling wasn't his only addiction. My banning his card playing didn't keep him from stopping in here for women and drink. Alcohol, that's what killed him, driving home dead drunk one night."

Anger rose in Jack. Poor Liane, trying to run the stately old hotel that had belonged to her grandfather under circumstances like that. Liane deserved better than some shoddy philanderer like her husband had been.

Jack scribbled his name and phone number on a napkin and laid it on the bar. "If you see anything of those bikers, would you give me a call?"

* * * *

Night had fallen by the time he arrived back at the Lucky Draw Hotel. Dim lights glowed from the lobby desk, and the smoke and smell of burning wood hung in the air.

Jack dreaded the thought of going up to his room, of the long, sleepless hours until morning. He'd just sit by the fire a while.

As he entered the dining room, he found Liane alone at a table, face turned from him toward the portrait of her grandfather and husband. When he spoke her name and she looked around, he saw that there were tears in her eyes.

He drew forward and sat down beside her.

"I've always wanted this hotel to be a good place, a safe place for people to enjoy."

"You've done a remarkable job keeping the hotel running," Jack assured her.

Liane glanced again at the picture. Jack's eyes followed hers to the handsome face of Robert Vale, frozen in time, with that smug, confident smile.

"He ruined everything," she said flatly.

By dying, Jack thought. False trust had left Liane blind to his faults, which according to Swenson were too numerous to catalogue. "I understand how you feel," Jack said, thinking of Darla. "When you build your life around a person, parting leaves a terrible void."

As if casting aside all thoughts of Robert, Liane stood up and with attempted brightness, asked, "Would you like some coffee?"

Jack caught her hand. He remained silent, gazing at her. "You must have loved him very much."

To his surprise Liane began to cry. "The very day Robert died, I had told him that I wanted a divorce." Her words were broken by choked, intermittent sobs. "You don't know what he was like. He twisted all the good in my life until it became some grotesque, ugly mess. He destroyed me, everything I cared about, bit by bit. I grew to detest him." Her voice rose. "I hated him!"

Jack reached out for her, gathering her gently into his arms. "No, you didn't hate him," he said softly. "You loved him, and he betrayed you."

He pressed Liane's face against his shoulder, his hand entangled in long strands of hair that gleamed red in the firelight.

23

To quell her tears, Jack drew her closer. He had intended the kiss to be the comforting one of some caring friend. He had not been prepared for the electric sweetness of her lips.

* * * *

In the huge room spotted with early morning diners, dishes were passed and coffee cups refilled, all automatically, void of the usual pleasantries. Midway through breakfast, Sheriff Morgan Spence entered, looking roughshod and weary.

"Two announcements," he said.

Liane's hand anxiously caught Jack's wrist. Mort, from where he sat at the next table between the Baker twins, exclaimed, "So, you've solved the case."

"Not exactly. First off, Dusty Pontier was shot with a .38 caliber handgun, which we haven't been able to locate. Any one of the three shots fired would have killed him."

"But who shot him?" Clint Baker asked, taking another forkful of hotcake.

"I've got one, good lead. The bikers he fought with at Swenson's Bar were spotted in Laramie *after* the shooting. I have an APB out for them now, so it's just a matter of time."

After he left, the spirits of the group rose significantly. Mort stood, wiped his mouth with a napkin, and said, "I, for one, am ready for a poker game."

"We don't have five players," Clint reminded him.

Mort chuckled. "Sure we do. That little gal seated right next you, Jack, would qualify as a pro."

"Will you fill the fifth chair?" Claude asked, disbelief sounding in his tone.

Liane gave polite reply, "I'll make some money arrangements and join you in the poker room in ten minutes."

Jack, surprised by her quick agreement, followed her into the lobby. "You sure you want to do this?"

"It might help everyone recover from their shock," Liane

said with a slight smile.

The game started short of idle conversation. Bets were pushed forward, bets of cash—the twins did not want to play with poker chips. Out of the corner of his eye Jack studied each of them in turn: Mort, affable and good-natured; the Baker twins, hard and cold-eyed; Liane, beautiful, but at the moment very serious and remote. His gaze shifted back to the twins. If any of this group had murdered Pontier, he'd lay his money on those two. He had noted how they worked together, no words needed, in practiced unison. He could picture them shooting Pontier, stealing and splitting the cash from the leather pouch.

"Fold," Mort said, abruptly turning Jack's attention from his thoughts back to the game. Jack stared at his own lousy hand. Not even two of a kind. He followed Mort's lead and tossed his cards face down on the table.

Claude raised the bet, and Clint and Liane stayed. A lot of money lay in the center. Jack hoped Liane knew what she was doing.

"Call," Claude said. Claude had two aces; Clint beat him with two pairs. Looking self-conscious, Liane showed her hand. Three of a kind for the win.

The next hour or so followed a similar pattern, with Mort and Jack falling further and further behind. Jack glanced at his dwindling funds, realizing he was going through the money he had borrowed from Liane with an almost out-of-control rapidity.

Mort looked from his dwindling stack to Jack's. "Guess we're on a losing streak, partner," he said.

Mort's words caused Clint's eyes to glisten. He now held the title of major winner. "Five hundred dollars says I've got the best hand," he announced, pushing money forward.

"You did that on purpose," Claude said angrily. "Just

because you know I don't have that much left."

"That's the name of the game, bro. Looks like you're out."

"Advance me some money," Claude said with great hostility.

"Afraid not," Clint replied. "What's yours is yours; what's mine is mine. I have it all; you have nothing. End of story."

"We'll see!" Claude sputtered. He jumped to his feet, the cards he held scattering in every direction. He headed to the door, turned back to glare at Clint, then stormed out.

"I'll see your bet," Liane said, "and raise three hundred."

"Two queens, and two kings," Clint said triumphantly.

Liane spoke in a quiet, demure way. "Three sevens and two fives. Full house. I guess Lady Luck is smiling on me today." Although she tried not to look elated, high spots of color appeared on her cheeks and sparkles danced in her amber eyes.

Jack, noting the almost innocence of her pleasure, was aware at the same time of Clint, a notoriously sore loser.

"Damn him!" Clint spat out. "Claude's to blame for this! He knows I never win unless there's five players at the table!"

Clint got slowly to his feet, facing Liane, his unblinking stare sending stabs of ice into Jack's heart.

A showdown, this time without guns, across the poker table. The first time Liane had squared off with the likes of Clint Baker. She would have no idea how ruthless, how dangerous, men like him really were. Jack's fear for Liane increased, he barely heard Mort's teasing voice. "Guess the poor little twin wants to win it all." Mort laughed shortly. "Doesn't even want to share with brother Claude. Doesn't even want a runner-up for his title."

* * * *

Three blasts, like cracks of thunder, immediately

followed one another. The pop of firecrackers, the backfire of a car—before a more deadly guess could spring to Jack's mind, his thoughts were curtailed by a woman's scream. Gunshots and Liane's wailing cry. Terror turned Jack's heart to stone.

Jack leaped from his bed, plunging forward through the darkness, wildly freeing himself from the tangle of covers. He raced into the hallway. The hall light had gone out, or, rather, had been shot out for he felt the sharp spatters of glass beneath his bare feet.

Someone leaned against the passageway wall. When he reached the form, bent over as if in pain, he recognized Liane. "My God! Are you all right?"

"I'm ok," Liane gasped. "But someone isn't. You heard the shots. I'm sure they came from Clint Baker's room."

Jack pounded on the door. "Clint? Clint, open the door!" He whirled to Liane, "It's locked. Do you have a key?"

"The doors all lock automatically when they are closed. I have a set of master keys." She scampered away from him toward the lobby. Jack met her on the stairway, took the keys from her, and returned.

His hands shook as he fumbled with the lock and swung the door wide-open. "Clint."

As he stepped inside, he was smacked with the odor of gunpowder. As he rounded the bed, he stopped short.

"What has happened?"

He reached Liane before she could draw any closer. "Go downstairs and call the sheriff."

Jack could hear her running steps, which soon vanished into deep, profound silence.

Clint and Claude Baker, as if in the tableau of some Western gunfight, lay some distance apart. He saw that Claude was dead without checking. He had been shot square in the forehead. He turned to the other, who lay face down, shot in the back. A snub-nosed revolver, the kind you could slip into the top of a boot, lay beneath his hand, as if he had tried to keep hold of it to the very end. It looked as if Claude had paid his twin a visit tonight, and had at some point during their argument shot Clint in the back. Clint had lived just long enough to wrestle the gun from his brother's hand and shoot him between the eyes.

As he drew closer to Clint, Jack spotted the card that lay face up on the floor beside the gun. The eight of clubs glowed evilly in the harsh, overhead light.

Jack found another card, the eight of spades, stuffed, half-hidden, into Clint's shirt pocket. He thought of the ace of clubs he had found instead of Dusty Pontier's cash. Three deaths. Three cards. What could this mean?

Mort's voice sounded from the doorway. "Liane told me what happened. Sheriff's on the way."

Mort strode into the room like some wild-west marshal. He stood, feet planted apart, surveying first Clint, then Claude. When he finally spoke, it was with amazement, "Damned if they didn't kill one another."

"It doesn't make sense," Jack said, "no more money than Clint won today."

"People have been shot for dollars and cents," Mort returned. "But in this case, there's probably much more involved. Like the money they stole from Dusty. These two were the worst that..." His words faded away. "What's this?"

"Better not touch anything."

Despite Jack's warning, Mort stooped and lifted the card the lay that near Clint, exclaiming, "The eight of clubs."

"There's another one in Claude's pocket, the eight of spades."

"What's going on here, Jack?"

"This isn't about money at all," Jack answered, realization pouring over him. "It's about revenge."

* * * *

Jack stood in front of the painting in the dining room. He looked from the figure of death lurking in the background to the men gathered around the card table. Then his gaze locked on the cards "Wild Bill" Hickok was holding the day Jack McCall had shot him in the back.

The low-spoken words from directly behind him, reciting lines from a poem in ghostly refrain, caused him to start.

"Two black eights, aces a pair, Dead Man's Hand—better beware."

Jack turned to face Mort. The thought had struck Jack before, but not with such an overpowering force: these crimes, the deaths of Pontier and the twins, were being played out in mimic of this infamous hand. Dusty Pontier had been left the ace of clubs, the twins, two black eights. This explained the appearance of the cards. Jack looked again at the hand Hickok held in the painting, clearly visible. Not four cards, but five, if the red one was counted, the controversial jack of diamonds, considered by many players to be part of the unlucky draw.

Five cards—five players. Of the five people who had played at their poker table, three were dead. Jack suddenly had no doubt the killer intended to carry out this pattern to the end. Two cards remained, the ace of spades and the jack of diamonds.

Jack could feel a sinking in his heart—one for Mort Jenkins and one for him.

Mort, unaware of Jack's horrible revelation, stood looking up at the painting, laughing a little, his habit, whether things went right or wrong. "Liane thinks the world and all of her grandfather. And of this painting, too. Her grandfather had it made to commemorate his winning of this hotel."

"I know. He won it in a poker game. She told me."

"Don't tell Liane I said this." Mort's secretive voice was broken by another short laugh. "But her grandfather would have to have been the biggest cheat in these parts. It would be some grand coincidence if the man who lost the hotel had just by *accident* drawn the exact same cards as 'Wild Bill' Hickok."

In the silence the eerie echoing of lines from the poem replayed. "Two black eights, aces a pair, Dead Man's Hand— better beware."

Mort's gray eyes twinkled as he continued to gaze up at the cards. Jack wondered how Mort could fail to make the connection, to look at those cards and not realize exactly what was taking place.

"Yes, sir, he was the biggest fraud of all," Mort went on. "That deal wouldn't come up once in a thousand years."

Mort started to say something else, but was interrupted by the entrance of the sheriff. Morgan Spence had been in and out of the hotel all morning, now he stomped into the room, looking grim and weary. "That little snub-nosed revolver wasn't registered to either of the Bakers."

Mort, with an arch of shaggy eyebrow, replied, "Did you expect it to be?"

"The way it looks..." The sheriff stepped closer to them. "Claude Baker shot out the hall light. The door closed behind him as he rampaged into his brother's room. He shot Clint in the back, but didn't kill him outright. Clint got the gun away from him and shot him in the head."

"Could have happened," Mort agreed.

"By the way, I've found those three bikers, but they're in the clear. So the Baker twins must have been the ones who waylaid Pontier."

"Then how do you explain the cards?" Jack asked.

"Everyone knows how superstitious they were. I think because they were twins, one carried the eight of clubs and one the eight of spades. Those cards had a special meaning for them, sort of like a talisman."

Jack shook his head. "I don't buy that."

Spence's lips pulled tensely downward. "You got a better explanation?"

Jack gestured to the painting. "Have you taken a look at the cards in Hickok's hand? Compare them with the cards we've been finding. They show the same kind of deep-rooted hatred over some great loss."

"What are you getting at?" Mort inquired humorously, "that the ghost of Jack McCall has risen from his grave and is killing again?"

"We might be dealing with a ghost," Jack said shortly, "only not Jack McCall's. Robert Vale's."

A hush fell over the two men. Mort had goaded Jack into saying what had flitted through his mind, what he hadn't had a chance to seriously consider. Now he had to go on with it.

Mort recovered before the sheriff. "You could be on to something, Jack. Everyone knows that Robert Vale was the biggest gambler around. It's common knowledge that he lost a small fortune at the table right before his wreck." Mort's eyes lit with enlightenment. "Yes, that may be the answer. Liane's husband could have faked his own death and right now is hiding somewhere in or around the hotel. Vale plans to reap vengeance on the poker players who ruined him."

"That's utter nonsense," the sheriff said.

"But it is possible," Mort pressed on. "He was burned beyond recognition, wasn't he?"

"Did you do any tests to make sure the body in the car was Vale's?" Jack asked.

"I didn't need to. The vehicle was registered to him.

Liane identified the watch and rings he was wearing."

"It would be easy enough to find some transient, a poor, lonely soul nobody would miss, and stage the whole thing," Mort declared. "And as for Liane, she could be in on it, too, if there was enough insurance money involved."

"If Vale's still alive, I'm sure Liane doesn't know it," Jack cut in defensively, not happy about the twist Mort had tagged on. He added solemnly, "But you're probably right, sheriff. We're getting way off the track."

"We do have to consider those cards," Mort reminded him. "You said so yourself. Just look at the facts. First Dusty Pontier is found dead with the ace of clubs in his pocket, then the twins, each with a black eight."

"Ace of clubs, eight of clubs, eight of spades. Only two cards left. The jack of diamonds and the ace of spades." Jack turned to Mort and finished, "One for you and one for me."

* * * *

"What about Liane? I understand she was playing poker yesterday," the sheriff said, "Wouldn't one of the cards be slated for her?"

Mort, as if he had missed the sheriff's sarcasm, answered seriously, "Other people kid Liane about being a card shark, so I took it up, too, but the truth is, Liane doesn't like card games. She just played yesterday to humor the twins. That's the only poker game I've known her to sit in on, so no one could possibly be seeking revenge on her."

"If you think that everyone involved in this game will be murdered," the sheriff said sourly, "then if I were you two, I'd clear out of here. Of course, you're not to leave the vicinity right now, but you could rent a nice, safe room in Laramie."

"I could never convince Liane to leave," Jack said, "so I'll just stay here with her. But you could, Mort, and I think you should."

"If this theory with the cards is right," Mort replied, "I won't be safe anywhere. Anyway," he added, like an old gunslinger holding his ground, "this is my home. And I prefer fighting to the death right here on my own turf."

During the hours they had spent together at the Lucky Draw Hotel, an affection of sorts had sprung up between Mort and Jack. Jack didn't want the old man to be in any danger. He attempted once more to convince him to leave. "The way I see it, you're at greater risk than I am. Why not do something to protect yourself?"

"Nope," Mort replied stubbornly. "I'm staying right here."

Jack felt a shadow of fear move over him. Mort was certain to be the killer's next victim. And no one, Jack included, would ever be able to protect him.

* * * *

Late that afternoon Jack wandered down into the dining room. He sat at the table near the fireplace, the one Liane and he always chose, and stared at his long-forgotten cup of coffee.

Jack hadn't noticed that Liane had entered until she slipped into the chair across from him. "Everyone's checking out."

"Except for Mort. It will take more than a triple killing to run him off."

"And you, too."

Liane smiled at him, a mixture of admiration and gratitude. Her expression caused him to recall the excitement of their first kiss.

"You're just like Mort, aren't you? You're both just like the fearless men who tamed the west."

She wouldn't have thought so if she could have seen him quaking in his boots as he had forced himself down the stairway last night. But he wasn't about to dispute her words or say anything to mar her image of him.

"I'm glad you're staying, Jack. You make me feel safe."

"No one's safe," he replied, trying to keep the grimness out of his voice.

"That's why I want you to have this." She reached into her large, canvas purse and passed a rusty old Smith and Wesson across the table to him. "This belonged to Grandfather. There's a full clip in it. It hasn't been fired for a long time. I hope it still works."

"Someone just rang the desk bell." She rose abruptly. "Another guest leaving," she said and quickly left the room.

Jack examined the revolver. Despite its age, he could detect no problem that would prevent it from working; satisfied, he rose and clicked the safety. The rest of the day Jack kept the gun tucked in his belt and hidden by his denim jacket. Even though his having a weapon would give him no leverage against a sneak who preferred shooting his victims in the back, it nevertheless made him feel secure, the way Dusty must have felt about the leather money packet he had always kept strapped close to his body.

The waning sun, blocked by the mountains, cast its last dim, gloomy light through the old hotel. The vacationers had one by one checked out. Liane had dismissed the help. Only a young woman named Sara, who worked in the kitchen, elected to stay, to share their uncertain fate.

Approaching night increased Jack's restlessness. Even though Mort, Liane, and the hired girl had all retired, he remained downstairs, wandering around the building. At midnight he went up to his room.

He, fully dressed, stretched out on the bed. The soft mattress did nothing to relax his tense muscles. He lay awake for hours before finally drifting into a light sleep, only to be jarred awake by a shrill ringing, that tore through him like an electric jolt.

He sat bolt upright. It took him a moment to identify the noise. When he did, he groped for his jacket and took the cell phone from the pocket.

Jack hadn't received a single call since he had crossed the Wyoming border. Who would be phoning him now, at this hour? The only one he had given his number to had been Swenson, the owner of the bar in Laramie.

Jack adjusted the talk button with nervous fingers. "Hello," he said tensely.

Someone remained on the line, but did not answer. He waited, then asked angrily, "Who is this?"

Whispered words he could barely make out, answered. "I'll be in the poker room."

"What...?"

Before he could finish his question, a click sounded.

Jack had been wrong. The killer's next victim was to be him instead of Mort. Jack stood up, clamoring into his boots. With the gun Liane had given him in hand, he moved to the door. There, he paused, wondering if this maniac would be downstairs, or waiting for him in the hallway.

Whatever Jack did, the man, set on seeing this ghastly scheme to the end, would come after him. Better he be the pursuer.

Pressed against the wall, Jack drew in his breath and swung open the door. He waited, but heard no sounds from the dark corridor. And, damn, it was dark. The overhead fixture shot out last night had not been repaired.

Hovering close to the left side of the hallway, he ventured toward the stairway. Ready to duck, hand tight against the trigger, he slowly descended the winding steps. The lamp from the desk glowed across an empty room.

He cautiously continued on toward the dining room. The

painting of 'Wild Bill's' last moments, highlighted by the overhead chandelier that burned day and night, had never looked so spooky. How could he be such a fool? He felt as if he were acting out some third-rate western movie, where the hero walks straight into an ambush.

Jack, scarcely breathing, wound around tables and toward the poker room. There he stopped short, holding the revolver in both hands, barrel toward the ceiling ready to lower and fire. But instead of entering, he stepped to the side, and flat against the wall, snaked a hand around the doorframe and switched on the light.

The sudden, brilliant glare illuminated the poker table, the bookshelves, the photos of the hotel in its hey-day. No place here for anyone to hide. He didn't step into the room, just whirled back, half expecting to be hit from behind with a bullet. But none came.

First, Jack checked the main entrance to the hotel, which he found securely locked. Then he took the ring of keys from behind the lobby desk and one by one searched all the rooms on the bottom floor. At last, still on adrenalin high, he returned to the lobby and came face to face with Liane.

Jack, as startled as she, lowered the gun barrel. He hadn't intended his voice to sound so harsh. "What are you doing down here?"

"I can't sleep. I keep hearing strange noises. I thought they came from outside, as if someone were trying to get in."

"It's just your nerves. Whatever happens, you need to stay in your room."

"Something…awful…is going to happen tonight, isn't it, Jack?" She stepped closer to him.

The scent of flowery perfume hung around her. She wore a pale yellow silk robe that brought out the amber flecks in her eyes. She had never looked more beautiful. Jack resisted the impulse to reach out for her, to enfold her tightly in his arms. But that wasn't the way to protect her. He couldn't afford to be off-guard, even for a second.

Jack told her about the caller's whispered words, "I'll be in the poker room."

"Do you think someone came in from outside?" Liane questioned. She didn't wait for him to answer. "I'm calling the sheriff." Liane headed to the desk phone, clicked it a few times, then turned to him, saying with disgust, "The line's been going out off and on ever since that storm. Right now it isn't working."

"I have a cell phone in my room. We'll use that."

"Before I came downstairs, I talked to Sara, so she's ok. But, Jack, have you checked on Mort?"

Jack hadn't even thought of Mort until now. With mounting fear, he strode ahead of Liane to the old man's door. Why had Mort's safety just occurred to him? The phone call that had sent him downstairs might have been a ruse, Mort tonight's target instead of him.

His tap on the door resounded in the stillness.

Jack's hand knotted into a fist and he pounded.

"What in the hell...who's out there?" a gruff voice called.

Jack, flooded with relief, said, "Jack and Liane."

Mort opened the door. In his long underwear, the way his mass of gray hair ruffled, made him look comical. But no humor glinted in his eyes, narrowed and cold. "Trouble?" he asked.

"We wanted to make sure you were ok," Liane said. "Jack thinks some outsider might have entered the hotel tonight."

Mort squared his shoulders belligerently. "I'll just get dressed and take a look around."

"I've already done that. I've checked everything." Jack filled Mort in on the details. "Liane's going to call the sheriff's office. They'll be sending someone out. We'll just all go downstairs and stay together until they arrive."

Jack went into his room to pick up the cell phone. The first object he saw was the card. The jack of diamonds lay sedately upon the white pillowcase, like a courtesy mint left by the maid.

Frozen, he stared down at the card, at the black, dotted eyes and the mustached face topped with red crown. Every detail leaped out at him, the flowing, yellow hair, like 'Wild Bill' Hickok's, only flipped up at the ends and stylized. Jack lifted the jack of diamonds, fear coursing through him. By some trick of light, the plastic face appeared to alter, to be grinning up at him, mocking him.

* * * *

Tonight's caller had summoned him downstairs in order to put this warning message in his room. Or was the killer tormenting him with the fact that he would be the next to die?

Jack woodenly joined the three, who waited in the lobby. Liane called the sheriff's department and they contacted Morgan Spence, who wasted no time arriving. He stood looking at the jack of diamonds Jack had handed him and without comment laid it on the desk.

"You say you thought someone entered from outside, but the doors were locked when you retired," he addressed Liane.

"That's right. But we didn't check the outside of the hotel to see how the intruder got in."

"My men did that first thing. No break-in occurred here."

"Simple reason for that," Mort spoke up. "Someone has a key. The ring hangs on a peg behind Liane's desk. Simple enough for someone to borrow it and make copies."

"Or else the prowler was already in the hotel." Spence's hard gaze shifted to Jack. "All the others who were left with a card were found dead, but no one tried to kill you. Does that seem odd to anyone but me?"

Jack could almost hear the sheriff's thoughts, see him reconsidering yesterday's claim that the twins had killed Pontier and one another. He must be concluding that Jack had shot all three of them and had dealt the jack of diamonds to himself to avert suspicion.

"Liane heard sounds from outside the hotel," Jack said.

A note of sourness was present in Spence's next question. "What you're telling me doesn't make sense, Handley. Why would some intruder enter the hotel in the dead of night for the sole purpose of making a phone call to you and leaving a card? I'd say the risk on his part would be greater than the advantage."

"He's playing a game," Jack replied just as sourly, "and this is part of it."

"The killer might be trying to get you to leave here," Liane said. "He is warning you, Jack, to stay out of this."

"If I know Jack, he's not going to go," Mort piped up affably, his gray eyes twinkling. His voice dropped lower and became pretentious. Aiming a finger at Jack as if it were a gun, he exclaimed, "Watch your back, Partner."

* * * *

Later that afternoon Mort Jenkins ambled into the dining room. "Suppose a cowboy can get a cup of coffee," he called over to Sara, before he took a seat at Jack's table.

"The sheriff just left," he said to Jack. "He's about as much help as a monkey on a trail ride."

"I've been doing a lot of thinking," Mort went on. "The damnedest things keep running through my mind."

"Like what?"

"Forgetting the idea that Vale is still alive..." Mort started, then stopped to gaze up at the painting of the famous 'Wild Bill' Hickok poker game.

Jack regarded it, too, the picture Robert Vale must have looked at every day after his marriage to Liane. Jack scrutinized the five cards—a dead man's hand because Vale was pretending to be dead.

"If Vale really did die in the wreck," Mort started again, "that means there's only three of us left. I'm not guilty and you're not. That leaves one other person."

Liane. Jack felt a dryness grip his throat. Already, before they had been verbalized, Jack found himself rejecting Mort's next words.

"Liane was devastated after Robert Vale's wreck, or so they tell me." He stopped talking while Sara brought the coffee. "Thank you, dear." Mort took a swallow before going on. "What do you think caused her husband's accident?" Mort answered his own question. "He got stinkin' drunk, a reaction to losing a fortune at the table. If you asked me, Liane probably got to brooding about that last poker game, got to pointing blame at the players. Without the slightest doubt, they had all worked together to cheat Robert Vale."

"How could you know that? You weren't in the game that night, were you?"

"I'm not dead. That should answer your question. Not yet, anyway. Dusty and the twins—the first and the worst of the group—were naturally settled with first."

"If what you're saying is true, it will end right there."

Mort sighed heavily. "I'm likely to be tagged as one of them. There's such a thing as guilt by association."

Jack made no reply.

Mort took another gulp of coffee, then used a napkin to wipe his mustache. "Liane's grief could have been too much for her, caused her to slip a gear, go out of control. Grief does some funny things to a person. In her case, it could have left her dead-set on revenge."

He set down his cup, and asked in a self-satisfied way. "What do you think? That just might be what this is all about."

Unable to come up with any sensible reply, Jack just stared at him. Of all things, he thought of Darla, about how his last inkling of love for her had vanished the moment she had betrayed him. After that, Jack thought he would never again trust another woman, and here he was, trusting Liane. He fought against an impulse to jump to his feet and demand that Mort take back those accusations. Instead he remained in stony silence.

After a while, with a short, amused chuckle, Mort qualified. "It's hard to believe that a sweet little gal like Liane, no higher than my shoulder, would be able to dry-gulch those three. They were the meanest, toughest characters a person ever laid eyes on."

"She didn't," Jack said quietly. "Liane told me that before her husband died, she was planning to leave him."

"What a woman says and what she feels... in here," Mort tapped his heart, "isn't always the same, you know that, Jack. Whether you want to believe it or not, what I'm telling you is entirely possible. It wouldn't be the first time a woman's made fools out of men." He finished his coffee in one loud sip. "'A word to the wise.' Just keep your guard up."

Liane couldn't be guilty. If she were, she wouldn't have given Jack her grandfather's gun the way she had. Or did she have some ugly, hidden reason for that? One like blaming this whole series of crimes on to him?

Mort leaned across the table on his elbows. "That card, doesn't it worry you?"

"The jack of diamonds may or may not be considered part of the dead-man's hand," Jack reminded him. "Some players only consider the combination of black aces over black eights as unlucky. I didn't play a single game of poker around here until I came to the Lucky Draw Hotel, and then I lost every time. The jack of diamonds may be an exemption card."

Both shaggy eyebrows lifted. "Do they give those out? I'd like one, myself."

Mort glanced from the painting of Hickok back to Jack. When he spoke again, his voice revealed no trace of fear, just of calculation. "In any event, all the cards have been played but one, the ace of spades. That one must be for me."

* * * *

In the poker room Jack opened the heavy wine-colored drapes and stared out into the darkness. A full moon high overhead made clear the road that would eventually fork upward to the rugged cliff where he had found Pontier. Jack knew he would never be free of that image, the twisted bike, the bullet-ridden body. Nor of the twins, the small, grotesque holes left by a snub-nosed revolver, ones that had caused immediate death, but little blood.

Jack felt the pressure of the Smith and Wesson in his belt as he shifted his weight and turned his back to the window. The shaded globe, bright on the table, cast eerie shadows along the edges of the room. Jack seated himself in the same chair where he had played poker. Of all things, he thought of Mort's suggesting to the twins and him that they all work together to cheat Pontier. When Jack had objected, Mort had passed it off as a joke, and maybe for him, it was, but what about the other three men? They played to win, any way possible, working alone or in unison.

Cheaters, big-time robbers, stripping some unsuspecting victim of their money, the way they had started to do with him. Heartless, vicious men—in the old days whoever shot down cheats like those three would be considered a hero.

Jack sat a while, thinking about that, then he rose and walked around the room, stopping to gaze at the photos on the wall. The first one showed the hotel, a prize from another age, glorious in its day, only under another name, The LaRoane Inn. The second portrayed Liane's aristocratic, silver-haired grandfather. Jack ambled on from picture to picture and stopped at a bookcase where a series of photo albums were marked by year. He took out the most recent and carried it with him to his spot at the poker table.

The book, belonging to Liane's husband, was crammed with photographs. Beneath the last picture someone, probably Liane herself, had written, *Robert's final game.* Jack studied it, one of the few group shots not taken in this room. In this game, probably played in back of some bar in Laramie, Robert Vale, according to Mort, had lost a sizeable fortune. Or had his losing been part of some overall plan made up to fleece someone else?

Jack stared at Robert Vale, not liking his fancy hairstyle, the too-perfect way he dressed, his oily smile. Next to Vale sat Dusty Pontier, looking pale and faded in desert camouflage jacket. Clint occupied the next chair, and to his left, as was the custom, his twin, Claude. Mort had spoken the truth—the old man hadn't been one of the five players in Vale's last game. On the end sat a burly young man Jack did not recognize.

Five men, the same number that played in Jack's poker games. Five players, five cards. Jack had been delivered the jack of diamonds. Now only the ace of spades remained. Jack had been given a card, but had not been killed. Why? What could that mean? Jack was struck with the only possible answer. If the ace of spades was to tag the next victim, then Jack was the dupe, the last man standing, the one to take the fall for all these crimes!

But who was left to perpetrate the operation? Jack stared down at the five faces in the photo again, this time remembering what Mort had told him about Liane and grief, about the possibility of Liane's blaming the players for her husband's drunken state that ended in his death, about her possible vow of vengeance.

Before this moment, Jack's suspicions had been tugs of unrelated facts buried in the hodge-podge of confusing events. Now they became solidified and focused. Jack closed the album, believing he had gleaned exactly what had taken place during and following Robert Vale's last poker game. "God, no," he said aloud.

Sara had gone home for the night telling Liane she would be back in time to serve breakfast. That left Liane, Mort, and Jack alone in the hotel. Jack hadn't been able to sleep tonight because of an intense feeling of forewarning. He had paced back and forth in his room, tense and fearful. *Tonight the ace of spades*, the words had funneled around him like a tornado, had prompted him to roam through the hotel and end up here.

It's certain, he thought. The killer intended to strike again tonight.

A shaking started in Jack's legs as he rose. He had delayed long enough, maybe too long. He had to get to the old man on time!

* * *

Jack rushed up the steps and raced along the dark corridor. The door to Mort Jenkins' room was ajar. Light fell in oblong pattern across the oak flooring in the hallway. Jack couldn't suck enough air in his lungs and felt light headed. A loud hammering had started in his chest.

He halted, gave the door a shove, peering in before he entered. "Mort."

The doors to the patio were open filling the room with cold, mountain air. Jack's gaze fell to the iron bed, spread with a patchwork quilt, then rose to the picture of an Indian, slumped on horseback still clutching his spear—"The End of the Trail."

"Mort!" Where could he be? Jack bounded toward the bathroom. Finding it empty, he swung back, this time seeing through waves of fear what he had not noticed before. On the cluttered nightstand beside the bed lay a single card—the ace of spades!

Jack became aware of a slight sound, a movement that disturbed the silence of the room like a ghost from some unsettled past. He whirled toward the balcony just as Mort stepped inside.

Mort looked from the card to Jack. "I reckon the killer did that all along, delivered the card first."

Jack stared at him unable to believe his brazenness. "You should know," he said quietly.

Jack had only guessed down in the poker room. Now he knew for sure. The fifth player, the one Jack hadn't recognized, was Mort's son. He could see the resemblance, the same burly form, the same deep smile lines around eyes and mouth.

Mort chuckled. "So you've figured it out, did you?"

"Yes. Your son, Mort Jr., didn't die in any hunting accident."

Mort's words flared with a hostility Jack wouldn't have thought him capable of possessing. "My son owed a huge gambling debt. I was forced to sell the ranch to pay it off, then with what remained, we planned to head out to California and make a fresh start. But instead of paying off the debt, Mortie joined Robert Vale's game. He was cheated out of all of the money I had gathered up for him. Mortie couldn't face me, went out into a field, put a rifle to his head, and killed himself."

Mort had given Jack the real story; only he had transferred the vengeful grief he himself had felt over to Liane,

45

trying to convince Jack that she was the guilty one. "I understand what you went through. You knew Vale had caught wind of your son's cash and had called in Pontier and the twins to help him get it. But to resort to this, how could you..."

For a moment Mort's face became hard and wrathful. "They destroyed my boy. They destroyed me. They all worked together, but they never will again. Vale died in that wreck before I had a chance at him, but I got the rest of them, got them good."

"What are you going to do now?"

"I think you can answer that, Jack." Mort's good spirits returned in a flash. He chuckled again. "I'm going to have to kill you now." He edged sideways as he spoke, closer to the nightstand and the drawer that must contain a weapon. "Didn't want to. Sort of got fond of you, boy, but it has to be. All along, I intended to leave you alive so I could blame the killings on you. But now I'll have to change my plans."

"If you kill me, who are you going to blame? Liane?"

"No, all along that little gal was slated for this ace of spades." Mort's eyes flickered downward, rested on the card for a second. "Had it all laid out and ready to deliver."

"But why?" Jack demanded angrily. "How could you blame Liane for what her husband did? How could you get her entangled in this web of hate and revenge?"

"I do hate her, Jack," he said, a hint of a smile remaining on his face. "You don't know just how much. She's here living the fat life in the hotel that should have been mine."

"How the hell do you figure that?"

"I got the whole idea from the dead man's hand," Mort said, amused, "and you haven't even guessed why. I'll tell you, then. Liane's grandfather cheated my uncle, my mother's brother, Ross LaRoane. He was the best damn friend a man ever had, took me in and raised me. But when he lost this hotel, he lost heart, was dead within a year. If it hadn't been for a dirty cheat," Mort exclaimed, waving his hand, "this grand old estate would have belonged to me and my boy."

"But Liane..."

"Guilty by association," he said.

"This is where your plot is going to fail," Jack told him. "Unless they know about the past, no one will believe any act of revenge would be directed at her."

"Wrong again, boy," Mort said exuberantly. "She played in our last game, if you'll remember. She bilked you out of a sizeable amount of money. The police will believe me when I tell them you were settling for your losses."

"I had intended to deliver this last card to Liane and leave myself clear out of it. The sheriff would have believed you spared me because I lost every game, didn't take a nickel of your money. By bursting in here, you spoiled your chance to live."

"To take the fall for you and spend a lifetime in prison."

"That couldn't be helped. By the way, I have already hidden Pontier's loot and the .38 I used to kill him in your room. The sheriff will find it there."

Jack still couldn't quite believe all of this. "You set me up good."

Mort agreed. "You've been hoodwinked. From the beginning."

"You had copies of the hotel keys. You got my phone number from Swenson and delivered the jack of diamonds to my room. You made sure you lost at our poker games, throwing down when you could have played, so, in the end, the sheriff would think you were being cheated, too."

"I did that, and more," Mort said. "Do you want to hear the best part? Dusty called the hotel while he was in jail trying to get a hold of the twins. When neither of them was here, he talked to me. Dusty was real excited about the cash you had gotten from your insurance settlement. I was the one who told him to invite you to our poker game. A nice touch, don't you think, having a Jack to take the blame when it's all over? Jack Handley, Jack McCall, jack of diamonds." He laughed. "Life's full of real irony, isn't it?"

Mort Jenkins was a madman. Stark grief, losing everything he held dear, had pushed him over the edge. But why did he look so sane, so sane and rational?

"If you asked me," Jack said. "It's all over."

Mort gave another of his short laughs. "No one's asking you. I'll shoot you and claim that you had come into my room to deliver me this ace of spades." As he spoke, he lifted the card from the stand. "I'll tell them you were going to kill me, but I got you, first."

"But the dead man's hand consists of five cards. And they've all been played, even the jack of diamonds. If the sheriff believes I was giving you the ace of spades, there's no card left for Liane."

Mort considered this, then answered cunningly. "True, I had intended to save the ace of spades for Liane. You made me show my hand early, but this won't spoil my plan. Since you weren't killed, the sheriff already thinks you only pretended to get the jack of diamonds to throw him off the track. The final card of the dead man's hand, the real jack of diamonds, will be found with Liane."

Mort opened the nightstand drawer. "I'm going to kill you now, Jack. Then go after the little lady. With no one here to stop me."

Jack's heart sank. The lines in Mort's face tightened with a deadly determination, the way they must have when he had tracked Pontier, when he had followed Claude into Clint's room, gunned them down, and shot out the hall light.

Jack had only one chance, to out-draw him. And he had a big advantage. The old man didn't know he had a gun. But would Jack ever be able to shoot him? As Mort's hand disappeared inside the drawer to lift out his weapon, Jack's own hand slid under his jacket. Nervous fingers tightened around the Smith and Wesson. Mort had started to lift the revolver, when Jack aimed and fired.

The bullet zinged into the side of Mort's revolver, just missing his knuckles. Startled, and jarred by the unexpected explosion, Mort lost his grip on the gun and it clattered to the floor. So, too, did the last card in the dead man's hand.

"Don't," Jack warned. "Don't even try to reach it. I don't want to shot you."

Sweat appeared on Jack's forehead. Mort was smiling at him, like a zealot willing to die for a cause. Not a chance in the world existed that he wasn't going to make a try for the weapon.

Jack had never killed a man. The only person he had ever even harmed had been Darla's boyfriend. But he would have to kill Mort. He had no other choice.

"Jack." Liane's frightened voice drifted in from the corridor. She appeared at the door, looking pale and stricken. "Jack, I heard..."

Liane's tone dropped, becoming barely audible. "Jack." She looked from the gun in Jack's hand, to Mort.

"See that ace on the floor," Mort said convincingly. "He came in here to kill me. I was to be his last victim." Mort's voice rose. "Now, girl, come over here, pick up that gun, and give it to me. He won't shoot you."

Both of them with guns—an old-fashioned shootout—that was what Mort wanted. Jack's finger poised on the deadly steel trigger. But he knew in his heart he would never be able to kill Mort.

"Don't listen to him," Jack said evenly. "He's lying."

Liane's amber eyes moved from Mort back to Jack.

"I'm telling you the truth, Liane. The minute you leave, he will mow me down me and then come after you. Jack Handley's as cold-blooded a man as I've ever seen."

Jack held his breath as Liane stepped forward. She bent and lifted Mort's weapon from the floor. She regarded Mort for a long, solemn moment, almost as if she intended to hand the gun over to him. Instead, she held on to it, lowering the barrel and carrying it with her to the door. "I'm going downstairs to call the sheriff."

They both listened to her steps growing fainter on the stairway. Jack kept his gun trained on the old man.

Mort smiled affably, saying, "It was worth a try."

* * * *

The Smith and Wesson Liane had given Jack had saved his life. When Jack had needed her trust the most, she had come through for him. He had known all along that she would. Maybe that was why he had fallen in love with her.

Jack and Liane watched the sheriff handcuff Mort Jenkins and read him his rights. Jack had liked the old man and the sight made him feel sick and empty inside. Mort had been born too late. Back in the old days, shooting cheaters would have won him applause, not a prison term.

Mort smiled at him. "Don't look so solemn, boy. The game's over, but I won enough to make it worthwhile."

Jack shook his head. "You killed three people, Mort, that's not a win. What you did was totally crazy." Jack turned to the sheriff, wanting him to understand. "Mort's grief drove him to this. Now, he's sorry."

"Sorry?" The old man chuckled. "I'm only sorry I didn't get to play all my cards."

THE DEVIL'S HANGMAN

The Devil's Hangman

Colorado Territory, 1874:

They had been pursued all afternoon and the day before, through hot Wyoming sun and dust, and everyone was growing weary. The bandits gathered around the small campfire, talking in muted whispers. From the sleeping roll near the rise of the cliff came an incoherent moan.

"He can't go much farther," the older one said. "He's hurt real bad. I doubt he'll make it through the night."

"We're all done for," the man beside him muttered. "They're hot on our trail. It's only a matter of time before they catch up with us."

At the first light of dawn they found their companion dead. Silently, the remaining bandits dug a rocky grave.

"What are we going to do now?" the older man said solemnly.

"I don't know. We're never going to make it out of this canyon with the gold."

Gold—lots of it. Drew gazed at the glimmering nuggets heaped inside one of the wooden crates he had just taken from the safe, and wondered why he felt no elation. Maybe it was the thrill of finding the gold that he had craved, not the actuality, not the grim problems that went hand in hand with such a glorious find. As Drew felt the coldness of the precious metal against his fingers, for an instant fear stole over him…like a forewarning of approaching danger.

Clearly, his partner, Tommy, didn't share his apprehension. "Just think of it, Drew—we're rich! You and I have hit the biggest strike ever made around Leland!"

The old swivel chair gave a tired squeak as Drew swung to the side and faced Tommy's big grin. Even though Tommy was only ten years younger than Drew, his tousled hair and sprinkling of freckles made him look like little more than a boy. Drew most of the time felt like his father. No wonder. He glimpsed his own face in the marred mirror behind Tommy—the lean, rugged features, the dour mouth that seldom smiled, hadn't since his wife had died over two years ago.

Tommy stepped closer, his eyes shining in anticipation as they fastened on the gleaming gold. "We can live the good life now. We can settle in some fancy-pants spot in Denver. We'll never have to work another day in our lives! We'll just sit around smoking cigars and playing blackjack."

Tommy made motions of placing cards on a table, one up, one down—re-enacting that night at the Red Elk Tavern when Drew had won this lucky claim in a card game. Usually this reminder, an ongoing joke between the two of them, lifted Drew's spirits, but today he remained grimly sober. "I want you to ride into Colorado Springs today," he said, "and make arrangements for Wells Fargo to send out a stage for the gold."

"What's the rush? And why go to all that bother and expense? Mid-week, let's just load it up and take it in ourselves."

Drew shook his head. "That would be asking for more trouble than we can handle. With those bandits back in town."

"We've been working out here for so long, poor as mice.

No one on earth would even suspect that we've struck it rich."

Tommy always accused him of being too suspicious, too cautious, so Drew didn't expect his next words to meet with the kid's approval. "No, I want it out of here, moved, safe and easy, with armed escorts."

"But I can't go today," Tommy returned. "This is Celene's birthday." He slanted Drew another of his big, lop-sided smiles. "You know how women are. I just can't walk out on her birthday. I'm inviting her to dinner tonight, right here in this cabin."

"She won't consent to being out here with you alone. It ain't proper."

"It is," Tommy countered, "if I include the old couple she boards with, those eagle-eyed Tates. Helga must be the world's best chaperone. Not that we need one." Merriment set a sparkle in his deep blue eyes. "My intentions are honorable. Tonight I'm asking Celene to marry me."

What a fool, Drew thought, swinging back to the safe. But who could talk sense to the love-struck? As far as that bold-eyed girl was concerned, Drew had from first sight got her number. Celene's interest in Tommy centered around one reason only—Tommy offered her a way out of the drudgery of working day after day at Tate's Mercantile. And now that Tommy had overnight turned into a very wealthy man, his need to be extra careful had increased three-fold. But try to tell him that.

"Your staying behind with all this gold is too risky," Drew said, the firm, father figure sounding in his voice. "I hear Reno Slade is back in these parts. And he's riding with Blackjack Logan and Joe Dodson. What do you think would happen if those three got wind of our strike?"

"No one knows about our good fortune, just you and me. That's the way you wanted it, and that's the way it is."

Tommy paused to draw in his breath, before adding adamantly, "And as for the trip to Colorado Springs, you're going to have to go yourself, Pard. I've got important business right here."

Business he'd be better off without, Drew thought, but said nothing. In the stillness he thought of Ella in her grave up on the mountainside. A woman just couldn't keep her love from showing, plain and clear, in her eyes, but in Celene's, Drew detected only falseness and pretension. Of course Tommy couldn't see the truth. And what did Drew's warning count for against flawless peaches and cream skin, wide blue eyes, and all that honey-blonde hair?

Tommy always chided Drew about his tendency to over-think everything, to make problems where none existed. He couldn't do anything about Tommy's upcoming marriage, but he could take action concerning this fortune the kid and he had sweated for month after dreary month. It must be removed at once, quickly, quietly, and safely.

"If I've got to go myself," Drew said in sour resignation, "then I'd best get started. I'll spend a night on the trail, and I'll be back tomorrow." Drew rose, put the gold back with the other cartons into the huge old safe he had procured from a going-out-of-business bank, and spun the combination.

There wasn't any real harm in this change of plans, in his making the trip instead of Tommy. They had nothing to fear from the Tates or from Celene, who even if she knew, would want Tommy to hang on to his newly found wealth.

Drew wondered if wariness had become too deeply ingrained in him. Nothing was likely to go wrong. Drew trusted his partner with his life, and the take from the claim, that no one even knew about, would be safe enough behind layers of steel. "You promise me, Tommy, that you'll take care—and not a word to anyone about the gold until it is far away from Leland, safe and secure in a big-city bank vault."

* * * *

By the time Drew had made final arrangements for the transport of the gold and left Colorado Springs, darkness had fallen. He headed north, winding through a tree-clad canyon toward the Wyoming border. He made camp beside a stream, lit a fire, and hovered close, for the night air at this elevation emitted an icy coldness.

Drew, except for the year before Ella had died with the fever, had been a loner, a foot-loose adventurer. Usually he relished the profound stillness of the vast, isolated mountains. Yet tonight he actually disliked being alone, a portent, he supposed, that he was going to miss Tommy. He had grown used to his jokes and laughter, his constant chatter. Drew even wondered if that were the real reason he opposed Tommy's marriage to Celene. His life would undergo another dreary change without the kid around.

Drew smiled a little as he unpacked his knapsack and began warming beans over the campfire and heaping coffee grounds into the small, blackened pot. As he boiled coffee, his thoughts remained on his partner. Kid, that's what Drew called Tommy although the boy was nineteen, going on twenty. A kid who loved to gamble, and had a knack for getting into trouble.

Drew had first seen him at the Red Elk Saloon in Leland trying to play cards with the big boys—that passel of bandits who rode with Reno Slade. Drew had watched the poker game from the corner of his eye that day, alert to trouble the way a forest animal senses danger.

"Lady luck is with me!" The boy puffed up like a bantam rooster, his crow just as annoying and as loud. This cocky young man with his fair blond hair, Drew thought, must be either a simpleton or a

stranger to have joined a card game with Reno Slade and his gang of renegades.

Reno Slade and Luke "Blackjack" Logan were dangerous men, but Joe Dodson was stupid to boot. Everyone knew Dodson, notoriously peevish about losing, always played with an eye for winning and one hand on the trigger. Those who won his money seldom lived to play a second round.

Still, Drew was a man who made it a point to mind his own business. He hunched over the bar and returned to his shot of whiskey.

"I win again!" Drew heard the crowing laugh, the scraping sound of a chair against the wooden floor as the boy rose to scoop in his bounty. He saw the bartender, not reliable Benton Farwell, but an old man he had left in charge, cast anxious glances in the game's direction and knew by the frightened look in his eyes that trouble was about to start.

"You little cheat!" Joe Dodson, with a sudden cry lumbered to his feet and grabbed the newcomer by the lapel.

"You dealt the hand," the wide-eyed boy cried with innocent indignation. He shook himself free from Dodson's clawing grasp and made a show of brushing at his shirt collar. "How could I have been cheating? Just tell me if you can."

"No one's that lucky." Dodson's eyes, dull and pale brown, fixed on the boy, then dropped to the full house, three aces and two queens that lay face-up on the table. "No one's that lucky," he repeated. "Isn't that right, Reno?"

"Probably pulled one of them aces out of his fancy shirt sleeve." Reno slid back the captain's chair, both hands on the arms, but remained seated. He regarded the kid through squinted eyes and said in a menacing tone, "We don't take any liking to cheats, do we, boys?"

The green kid's voice rose in protest. "I'm not a cheat!" He pointed a finger at Joe. "But you're a liar!"

The wrong thing to say. Drew heard rather than saw the cold click of steel as Joe Dodson drew his Colt .45. "Nobody calls me a liar!"

The boy's face paled. "Look. I don't want any trouble." Seeing that he was outnumbered, he took the money he had won and tossed it back down upon the table.

The boy began to step away when Reno Slade's booted foot snaked out, tripping him. Slade threw back his head and laughed as the boy fell flat on his face.

Slade, features obscured by dirty, sand-colored beard, was a giant of a man with fists as large as hams. His pride and joy were his boots, big boots of tan cowhide with red toes flanged with black and expensive Mexican spurs of etched silver. Boots that he often used to kick, stomp, and maim.

The third man, Blackjack Logan...a personal enemy of Drew's ever since Drew had won a gold claim from him and his brother in that card game a while back...watched with hawkish interest. "Where are you off to in such a hurry?" he mocked the boy. "We're not done with you yet."

The kid attempted to retrieve his dignity as he struggled to his feet. Drew was a man who disliked confrontations, but the unfairness of three against one rankled his sense of justice.

Drew watched the kid's face, the way the corners of his mouth, once marked by that devil-may-care grin, now quavered. "I swear I wasn't cheating!" The kid's eyes looked wide and frightened now as if it had just struck him that he was going to die. "Anyway, I gave your money back, even though I won it fair and square." He spoke with the naivety of one used to dealing with people who valued fair play.

Reno Slade tossed back his head and laughed again, then grew deadly serious, his features tightening into a mean, merciless leer. With his eyes still on the kid, he nodded to Joe Dodson. "Shoot him."

Dodson aimed the Colt at the boy's chest. Before he had time to fire, Drew lunged from the barstool. The suddenness of Drew's action took Dodson by surprise. Still he was able to pull the trigger before Drew could wrest the pistol from him. The shot missed its mark, skimmed past the kid, and lodged into the bar.

Disarmed, Dodson was no longer a threat, but the other two rose almost in unison. Drew looked from one hard face to the other. He could always read people by their eyes. This special skill of his had saved him on many occasions, but it would be of little help this time. Even taking into account Blackjack's personal grudge against him, a quick glance told Drew that Slade was by far the more dangerous of the two. He would go for him first.

Yet he could tell by the look in young Blackjack Logan's eyes that he intended to back Slade up. Whatever he did, whichever one he took out first, the other would kill him, and probably the boy, too.

The kid, frozen with fear, would be of no help. The old bartender gaped, as if he had gone deaf and dumb. Drew faced this fight alone. He couldn't win, but sure as he was standing here, he would take one of these worthless outlaws to the grave with him. Drew lifted Dodson's .45, finger poised on the trigger. At the same time Reno Slade went for his gun.

At exactly that instant, a gruff, commanding voice demanded, "What's going on in here?"

All eyes turned toward Sheriff Jeff McQuede. No doubt summoned by the sound of the stray shot, the sheriff stood blocking the doorway.

"Nothing, Sheriff," Slade answered calmly. "Just a friendly game of cards."

The big, rugged sheriff gave Reno a long and angry stare. "You know you and your boys are not welcome in this town, Slade. Now, I want you three to ride out. And don't come back. If I see you around here again, I'll lock you up and throw away the key."

As Reno Slade left, he turned back and glared at Drew. "You're a dead man," he spat. "Next time we meet, I'll be standing over your grave."

As soon as the savage trio left, the kid appeared to recover. "You saved my life," he said with great awe. "Who are you, anyway? What's *your name?"*

"Woodson. Drew Woodson."

"Tommy Garth." He gave Drew a hardy, grateful handshake. "Have a drink with me. I reckon I owe you one."

Since that day he had stepped in and saved his life, the kid had thought of Drew as some kind of hero. Hero, not the right label for a man like him. Tommy had taken to trailing along with Drew, and they soon became partners, working the old claim which had once belonged to Silas Tate and which Drew had won earlier in a card game with Blackjack. Everyone thought the claim had run out years ago, but the two of them, laboring like demons day and night, had uncovered a final, rich vein.

Wealthy beyond belief, that's what they were now. Then why wasn't he happy? Would joy follow once the gold, already weighed and crated, was secure in a bank vault in Colorado Springs?

* * * *

As Drew neared the cabin, his gaze fell to a trail of blood. His heart sank as he slid from his horse and rushed to the front door. The safe gaped open, totally empty. Tommy's revolver lay on the desk beside it. Drew moved woodenly forward and checked the chamber, knowing before he did, that it had been drawn, but not fired.

He had caused Tommy's death himself! The knowledge made him grip the edge of the desk for support. He had known better than to leave him behind with all this gold. Those bandits must have known about their find, must have been watching as Drew had ridden out. And the kid...staggering pain swept over Drew. It started as a sickness in the pit of his stomach and culminated in raw anger that caused a fierce pounding in his temples.

No telling how much time had elapsed. By now they had a

tremendous head start, but Drew would track them down, if it took the rest of his life! He made a quick search around the vicinity of the cabin. Some of the wheel tracks were too large to have been made by Tate's buggy. The numerous horses' hooves imprinted on dirt and grass led him to believe there were three or four bandits.

He would ride out at once, but first he must notify Jeff McQuede, so the sheriff could form a posse. Drew raced the roan down the wooded trail that wound down the mountainside into Leland.

Silas Tate had been watching from the huge window with the painted sign that read Tate's Mercantile. The owner, short, squat, bewhiskered, stepped outside, calling and waving his hand. Drew reined his horse up beside him.

Drew started to tell him what had happened, but Silas cut him short.

"I know. I told the sheriff I would wait for you, and we'd be catching up with the posse."

He looked older today, his face wrinkled in the bright light, his eyes narrowed. "I can't understand any of this," he said. "I suppose it's the result of some grudge against Tommy."

"No, we were robbed," Drew told him. "We hit a big strike and had a safe filled with gold."

"A big strike," Silas repeated. His eyes became large and rounded. "On that old claim of mine?"

"Yes, but it's gone now. They took it all."

"I saw the robbers, Drew," Silas said uneasily, "but I wasn't armed, so I couldn't chase them down. I headed back to town and got McQuede. I told him what I'm telling you. I saw a wagon pulling away, and three men on horseback. I don't think I could have done anything to stop them."

"You did what you had to do. You had to protect the

women."

Drew glanced toward the store where Silas' plump wife, Helga, peered out at them. Behind her, obscured by shadows, he could see Celene.

"They weren't with me then, Drew. I had already taken them home. Helga forgot her sewing basket, the one where she keeps her money tucked away. She insisted that I go back after it, so after I let them off here, I rode back out."

Silas' head bowed as he stared at the ground, leaving in view only his mass of graying hair and his snow-white side-whiskers. Even in this sad, meditative pose, he managed to look hard-hitting and tough.

"They headed off on the old Dexter road. One of the men was slung, stomach down, across a horse."

"That must have been Tommy," Drew said, his tone a mixture of agony and anger.

"They probably shot him right off," Silas agreed, "but why do you suppose they took him along?"

Drew was thinking they had taken Tommy as a hostage. Before he could answer Silas, Celene stepped outside. The sunlight made her look all glittery and golden and caused another sense of foreboding to steal over him.

"Drew, what happened? I told Tommy not to go over to that tavern and hang out with that crew over there." Her eyes brimmed with tears. "He made enemies, didn't he? Oh, poor Tommy!"

Helga, wiping her hands on an apron, hurried out to embrace Celene. "There, there, don't cry now. Just come back inside. Drew's here. He'll find Tommy. You wait and see. In the meantime, you and I will just stay here and send our prayers with them."

Drew turned back to Silas. "Did you recognize any of them?"

"Too dark," Tate said, with a shake of his grizzled head.

"Does the sheriff have any idea who he's chasing?"

"I reckon not. There's lots of robbers in these parts."

"But I can think of one in particular, one who might be keeping an eye on our claim."

"You mean Luke Logan—Blackjack?"

"If he's back in Colorado," Drew said, "he's bound to have stopped by the Red Elk Tavern. Since we need to know what we're up against, before we ride out, I'd best have a talk with Benton Farwell."

* * * *

The day Drew had won that mining claim in a blackjack game with Luke "Blackjack" Logan, he had felt on top of the world. He had viewed this event as a turning point, the lucky draw that would change his life forever. It had, but only for the worse. The disastrous reality of Tommy's death hit him full-force as he stepped from the bright street into the darkened barroom.

The Red Elk Tavern, a throwback to Leland's gold-rush days when the town was over-flowing with fortune seekers, still bore a look of grandeur. The huge, plate-glass mirror behind the bar reflected the red-draped windows and the scattering of expensive walnut tables. At one in center four men, silent and tense, played poker. At the end of the bar Blackjack Logan's brother, Walt, sat alone, slowly sipping a drink from a long-stemmed goblet.

Drew halted. He stared at Walt Logan, a tall, thin man, with intelligent near-black eyes and an educated, sedate manner. Walt Logan knew, without doubt, Blackjack's whereabouts, even the location of his infamous hideout, which Drew suspected sat just across the border in the Wyoming territory. He was, after all, the older brother, who used to ride with Blackjack as he robbed and terrorized.

Walt Logan had an education, had studied law back east, still Drew wondered if Walt Logan had really left the gang and gone straight, or if Blackjack just had need of a front-man to help him dispose of his ill-gotten gains.

"Are you looking for me?"

"No," Drew said, turning away, "for Benton Farwell."

Drew had no sooner spoken the tavern owner's name, than he appeared from a room behind the bar. His was another image that didn't fit, a gentleman, out of place in this rough and tumble setting. Benton Farwell, always so elegant with his carefully styled, tawny hair and his large, dreamy eyes of the same color. Always over-dressed too, down to the expensive onyx ring with the carved face of a knight. Today he wore a fancy white shirt and for a touch of casualness, a buckskin vest. All this glamour made him stand out in sharp contrast from his clientele, from the dusty cowboys and the scantily clad barmaids.

"I need to talk to you," Drew said to him. "Privately."

"Whatever you have to say to him," Walt Logan responded, "you can say in front of me."

"All right. I'm looking for Blackjack. Is he in town?"

"My little brother and I parted ways once he started hanging out with Reno Slade and Joe Dodson." Logan's eyes had grown a shade darker and didn't waver. "As I see it, a man's only as good as the company he keeps."

Drew remembered Walt Logan in his outlaw days, his black beard and long mustache, now he was clean shaven, yet the old image remained in his hard eyes, black as coal.

Drew stared at him. Instead of detestation, a moment of recognition flashed between them, the kind that like-minded men are sure to note in one another. Blackjack's brother possessed the same qualities as Drew, a cautious, calculating manner that at times Drew wished he could shake. Moreover, the over-protectiveness Walt Logan had for his kid brother differed little from the way Drew ran interference for Tommy.

"I heard Reno Slade and Dodson are back in Leland," Drew said.

Benton Farwell, who had come around the bar, spoke up mildly. "They were in my establishment yesterday afternoon. Dodson was drunk and unruly, so I asked him to leave. Reno Slade and Blackjack stayed. When your young friend, Tommy Garth, came in, Reno and Blackjack went right over to his table."

"Did you hear what they said?"

"I didn't catch a word of the conversation," Farwell replied in the same quiet way. "But it was serious."

"Did they leave together?"

"No. Tommy left first. The other two stayed here for an hour or so."

"Why do you suppose they were talking to Tommy?" Drew asked the question more to himself than to them.

"Doesn't mean a thing," Walt Logan answered. "Blackjack's friendly, that's all. He never likes to see anyone drinking alone."

* * * *

Drew turned on his heels and walked out of the saloon. Silas Tate was mounted, ready to head out. They rode side by side down the dusty street. Drew slowed as they reached the grove of trees just beyond the blacksmith's shed. He shaded his eyes and looked back toward the saloon, still clearly visible through the scraggly branches.

"What's wrong, Drew?" Silas asked.

"Reno Slade and Joe Dodson, with Blackjack as their leader, pulled off this robbery," Drew replied with certainty.

Silas' gray horse as anxious to be off as his owner, shuffled nervously as Silas reined to a stop. "I think you're right. When I went back to your cabin, I spotted four men in the distance, one driving a wagon, three more on horseback. They had Tommy slung across a saddle."

Excitedly, Silas went on. "Everyone thinks Reno Slade's the worst of the lot, but that doesn't include me. Blackjack Logan is the very devil himself! I knew the minute you ended up with my old claim, that you'd won it from one hell of a sore loser. Logan's been itching for a chance to get even with you ever since that card game."

"Instead of catching up with the posse," Drew said, "let's lay low and follow Walt Logan."

Silas hesitated, his eyes darting back to the tavern, then down the road the posse had taken, as if anxious to be off. "If he doesn't know anything, we'll be wasting time. He might stay in there drinking all day."

"Let's wait and see if he comes out."

They dismounted, leading their horses deeper into the trees. In no time Walt Logan emerged from the tavern. They watched as he, at a slow pace, headed off in the direction of his cabin.

"He's going home," Silas said, disappointed.

Drew remained silent as Logan, not even glancing in their direction, passed by them. "Let's just follow him and see what he does."

Drew let Silas take the lead. He'd been an army scout in his younger years. There wasn't anyone who could track and follow better than Silas Tate.

Silas cut off from the main trail, descended a steep slope, and followed Ames Creek, half dried up from lack of rain. As if Silas had a sixth sense, they forged as if invisible ahead of Logan and reached his house first, waiting in the forested area on the other side.

A nice spread, Drew thought, not like his own crude, log cabin, or the makeshift shacks that had sprung up outside Leland. Drew and Silas silently watched as Walt Logan slipped from his saddle and strode inside. A few minutes later, lugging a knapsack, he returned to the waiting horse. He galloped toward the old Dexter road.

They followed at a safe distance. After a while Walt Logan headed across low country, thick with sagebrush, toward the barren hills in the distance.

Silas put up his hand. "We have to wait now," he said.

"But we'll lose him."

"He'll pass through the canyon into Wyoming. Just give him time."

The sun had begun to beat down on them mercilessly, making the waiting that much harder. Drew reached for his canteen, took a long drink, then handed it to Silas.

After a spell of alert watching, Silas said, "Now."

At top speed they crossed to the foothills, which little by little joined with the jagged, granite outcroppings of the Rockies. Rumors abounded that bandits inhabited this area that they watched from the spot where the mountains opened into a narrow canyon. A perfect place for Blackjack to hide out.

Drew approached the cliff-like opening with a sense of dread, but Silas spurred forward eagerly. No shots rang out. They safely stopped again, Silas gesturing for Drew to dismount and follow him on foot.

They climbed the stony ridge where they soon spotted Walt Logan. He, too, was on foot now. He wound his slow, careful way downward, until he was midway to the canyon's floor. There, he stopped. His low, drawn-out whistle rose eerily upward.

As if waiting for the summons, Blackjack appeared.

"The devil!" Silas' words escaped his lips like an angry curse.

Blackjack Logan's curly black hair looked rumpled and dusty; his long mustache seemed to droop. He moved tiredly from between two high slabs of rock.

Drew could barely hear Silas' muffled growl, "Let's get them."

"Not yet. Let's get closer and listen. We may be able to find out what happened to Tommy."

Silas again led the way. Drew followed, his steps falling as stealthily as his companion's. They crept cautiously forward until they stood just above the two brothers.

"Brought you something to eat," Walt Logan was saying.

"About time." Blackjack ruffled through the bag his brother handed him and began to chew greedily on a hunk of meat. He wiped his mouth, and said with a beaming smile, "I was getting powerful hungry. Was thinking I'd have to snare me a rabbit."

"Damn fool. I ought to let you starve." Walt's tone was censorious, yet marked by gruff affection. "Fact, I ought to let them hang you."

"You know what they say." Blackjack quit eating long enough to grin. "Blood's thicker 'n water."

"I just ran across Drew Woodson at the Red Elk. He's hot on your trail. And he's got blood in his eye because of Tommy Garth."

Blackjack laughed defiantly. "I ain't afraid of him. He's honorable, ain't he? An honorable man can't do battle with someone as crafty as me! Anyway, as long as he thinks that no-good friend of his is alive, I'll be safe from him."

Walt frowned as he watched Blackjack upend the whiskey bottle. "What did happen out there, brother?"

"Tommy got himself shot."

The bandit's words, spoken so matter of factly, struck Drew like an arrow in the heart.

"Strangest thing," Blackjack said. "Another man was hidden at Woodson's cabin and he shot at us. Couldn't have been Woodson, because we followed him a while until we knew for a fact that he wasn't going to return any time soon. Someone else besides us was after that gold, Walt."

"Maybe Woodson got wind of your plans and turned back. Believe me, this Drew Woodson is no one to joke about. As sure as I'm standing here, he means to make you pay."

"Make me pay! He's the one who stole from me! You know that big strike should be mine," Blackjack said. "He cheated me out of my claim."

"You gambled away that claim, fair and square."

Blackjack laughed again. "Fair and square! Where did you learn words like that? You don't even talk like my brother anymore. You talk like some fancy pants preacher."

"Even you should know that tying up with the likes of Reno Slade again is a fool thing to do."

"The boys are just helping me even the score."

"No good will ever come of this. Why don't you turn yourself in before you get killed? I'll defend you. You could get off easy."

"The town will be up in arms about Tommy Garth. I ain't risking no hangman's noose. I'll just stay out here. Lay low."

"Maybe some day you'll grow up, Luke," Walt Logan said sadly, "that is, if it's possible for me to keep you alive long enough."

Blackjack's voice lowered, matched his brother's in sincerity, "Listen, Walt, I know where Reno stashed the gold." He waved his hand. "Not now, it's too dangerous. But soon I'm going after it. Then I'm heading off to Mexico. You coming with me, Walt?"

"You stay put tonight," Walt said in lieu of an answer. "I'll bring you more supplies tomorrow."

Silas raised his shotgun just as Walt Logan began to climb up the slope.

Drew placed a restraining hand on the barrel, saying softly, "Just let him leave."

Drew waited, absorbed in listening, catching the faint clomps of horse's hooves until they were lost in total silence. "Let's go," he said. This time he led the way down to the robber's hideout.

Alerted to the sound of their approach, Blackjack called, "Is that you, Walt?"

"You're surrounded," Silas shouted.

Drew's words followed. "Don't make a move if you want to live."

With catlike speed Silas un-slung the shotgun from his shoulder and aimed it at Blackjack. At this range he would kill him with one shot. Silas' hand began to tighten on the trigger.

If Drew were going to stop him from killing Blackjack, he had to act quickly. He whirled, striking the gun in an attempt to change the course of the bullet. His quick movement, unexpected by Silas, jolted the gun from his grasp. It spun on the ledge and slipped over the embankment.

Silas started to slide down the slope after it. At the same time Blackjack bent low, his hand moving swiftly to his boot. "Look out!" Silas cried. "He's going for his gun!"

A small, silver-barreled Derringer gleamed in the sunlight. Blackjack started to raise it, but Drew spun to face him. The loud click of his firearm, ready for action, momentarily stopped Blackjack. Intending to hit him with the rifle butt, Drew lunged forward. Blackjack had anticipated this and made a grab for Drew's weapon. As Drew tried to stop him, he lost hold on his rifle and it thudded to the ground. The two of them grappled for control of Blackjack's deadly little gun.

Silas circled them, taking position behind Blackjack. He wrested Blackjack's arms behind him. As soon as Drew took control of the pistol, Silas let go of the bandit and stepped away.

Blackjack stood facing Drew. Light wavered across his face, made him look as if he were smiling. He had killed Tommy, or at the very least he had caused Tommy's death. And what did he care? Drew's finger tightened on the trigger.

"Shoot him!" Silas yelled.

For an instant Drew thought he was going to do just that. But something Walt Logan had said a while ago stopped him, "Maybe someday you'll grow up." It caused him to see, instead of Blackjack, just a kid like Tommy, inexperienced, full of youthful arrogance. His hand remained frozen, immobile. He had never shot a man down in cold blood, let alone a mere boy.

"Kill him!" Silas snarled.

"Why should he? I didn't shoot Tommy and no one who rode with me did. The bullet that struck him came from someone hidden in the bushes beside the cabin."

Blackjack had made the same claim to Walt. Was it possible that they were dealing with yet another bandit? Drew's gaze shifted to Silas.

"Stop his lying mouth!" Silas burst out.

Blackjack was smiling now. This time Drew was sure of it. Drew's hand remained fast and tight against the trigger.

"He's not going to kill me," Blackjack said with great confidence. "I'm the one who can lead him to Tommy."

"We don't need you," Silas returned.

"You owe me, Woodson. Your buddy's alive only because of me."

Drew's jaw clenched. Blackjack had already all but told Walt that Tommy was dead. Now he was trying to save his own skin.

"Tommy was hurt," Blackjack said. "Reno was going to finish him off, but I stopped him. We took him along with us."

"Get the rope off my horse, Silas, and tie him up."

Drew kept his gun trained on the outlaw until Silas had bound his hands.

"This makes us even," Blackjack said, grinning at Drew. "I spared Tommy's life; you've spared mine."

"Shut up!" Silas ordered. "He might want to spare you, but I don't." As Silas spoke, he pulled a knife from his belt. "Tommy was going to get married, did you know that? Celene is just like a daughter to me, and now her heart is broke." Silas' face had gone white, menacing and cruel. He grabbed a handful of Blackjack's curly hair, thrust his head back, and set the blade to his throat.

"Don't do it, Silas," Drew said. "Let's just turn him over to the law."

Silas' voice became deathly quiet. "I know you're a little squeamish, Drew. Why don't you just go on back to town? Leave me alone with this filthy beast. I'll make him talk. I'll carve him up just like I did those Indians that attacked my place. Before I get through with him, he'll be begging to tell where Tommy is and what he did with the gold."

"No, Silas. I won't let you harm an unarmed man."

"I wish I had found you out here by myself," Silas said. As he spoke, he ripped the blade across Blackjack's neck, causing blood to trickle down across his shirt.

Drew stepped forward. "No, Silas. Leave him for the law."

"You should be grateful I don't finish you here and now," Silas said, brandishing the knife inches from Blackjack's face before returning it to his belt. "As it is, we're just saving you for the hangman's noose."

"You keep an eye on him," Drew said to Silas. He skirted the area looking for signs of wagon tracks and hidden gold, but he found nothing. After a while he returned, leading Blackjack's horse, and started toward the hideout.

"No use looking for the gold here," Blackjack said, drolly watching.

Drew approached the opening between the rock walls where Blackjack had first appeared. He wedged himself between the boulders and peered straight down to where jagged stones opened into a dim, tiny area about the size of a closet.

The perfect hideout—Drew would never have on his own found this little cavern tucked away in this isolated canyon. The large crates couldn't be stowed here, but the three men could have divided the best of the loot and left the ore hidden somewhere. Drew eased himself into the little cave and examined the area, but all he found was a sleeping roll, a worn jacket, and some black remnants of a small campfire.

On the way back to Leland, Drew rode alongside Blackjack with Silas bringing up the rear, his shotgun aimed at the outlaw's back.

"I wasn't lying about Tommy," Blackjack said. "He was hurt real bad when I left, but he wasn't dead."

"You said you could lead me to him."

Blackjack slanted Drew one of his egotistical glances. "That's not exactly true. But I can tell you he's with Reno. Reno thought we'd have a better chance if we split up. He wanted me to ride fast, leave a big trail. He and Tommy stayed with the wagon." His black eyes glinted in the sun. "I don't know what became of your big strike either. Reno said we'd divide it later."

Drew had heard him tell his brother he knew exactly where to find the gold. No use questioning him. Everything he said was going to be lies. "So you think Tommy is still alive."

"Joe Dodson hated him, for sure. But Reno wanted to keep him safe. He always likes to have a hostage just in case things don't go his way."

Once they reached the outskirts of town, before they passed the Red Elk Tavern, Benton Farwell and a few of his rugged clientele stepped out into the street. Several of them shouted at Blackjack, one voice ringing above the others, "Let's get a rope and hang him!"

Blackjack's dark eyes shifted in their direction, but he showed no sign of fear.

Several rough-looking men began to trail after them.

"Now, boys," Benton Farwell said in that quiet voice of his, "we don't want any violence. Let's let the law take care of him."

"With that no-good brother for a lawyer, he'll never hang unless we hang him ourselves!" a voice protested. The group once again surged forward.

"Stay back!" Silas warned, backing the saloon owner up.

Drew was grateful for his presence. The men always listened to him. There was no one he'd rather have riding shotgun than Silas Tate.

Still the hostile group, which could easily become a mob, caused him to speed the pace of his horse. Faces began appearing in storefront windows, bearing the same open expression of vengeance. Drew only wished rough and ready old Jeff McQuede would be at the end of their trek, so they could turn their charge over to him instead of to his young deputy.

"Don't be worrying so much, Woodson," Blackjack was saying. "I know Reno plans to keep Tommy with him. That's what he told me before I left him."

Drew felt his heart plummet. A heartless killer like Reno Slade, on the run, would not burden himself long with an injured hostage, especially a witness to the crime.

He had no other choice than to face the truth—by now Reno Slade had murdered Tommy, that is, if the kid hadn't been killed by Blackjack himself right from the very start.

Drew cast the bandit a long, hard glance. He hated everything about him, his impudent smugness, that innate treachery. As McQuede's deputy led Blackjack into the jail, the feeling settled over Drew that he had made a bad call by bringing Blackjack back to Leland. He should have let Silas Tate shoot him.

* * * *

As much as he dreaded the task, Drew must talk to Celene. Tommy would have wanted him to be kind, to do all he could to help her. It fell to him, as Tommy's best friend, to prepare her for the fact that Tommy was most likely was dead.

After a lonely evening meal he rode into Leland and stopped by Silas and Helga's home where Celene boarded, a neat, rock house with a high-fenced yard that set next to the store. No one answered his knock, but he noted that down the street around the church, a crowd had gathered. He headed toward it.

The pews inside were filling fast, and people were still arriving. On the wide porch near the doorway, Walt Logan stood apart from the others idly smoking a cigar.

Drew spotted Silas and Helga on the steps of the church, and ducking around a group of people, he caught up with them before they reached the entrance. "What's going on?"

Walt Logan answered for them, "A prayer meeting. Looks like the whole town's here." He took a deep draw on his cigar, and added, "praying for Tommy Garth."

Despite the fact that Logan sounded sardonically low-key, Drew didn't miss the undertones of deep hostility. Obviously he didn't blame himself for his lack of caution in leading them to his brother's hideout. Instead he blamed Drew for second-guessing him, for turning Blackjack over to Sheriff McQuede's deputy to be locked behind bars.

As Drew met Logan's cold, level gaze, anger flared, almost blinding him. "It's not going to do much good, is it? Not when your brother and his two henchman shot Tommy down in cold blood."

Helga let out a little gasp, and Silas, hand tight on her arm, led her inside.

"Don't be saying what you can't prove," Walt Logan replied, his words slow and certain, as if he were addressing a witness for the prosecution. "There's been no body found, so according to law, no one's been killed."

Tommy had probably been dead from the very start. Instead of taking a live hostage, they had thrown Tommy's body across a horse, to be tossed in some deep ravine where he would probably never be found to avoid a charge of murder if they were captured.

"Did it ever occur to you," Walt Logan asked, "that your young friend might have wanted all the gold for himself?"

"Why not share with me instead of with three bandits?" Drew clipped back.

"You don't understand the working of the criminal mind," Logan replied with a slight smile, "not the way I do. Tommy never intended to share, but to let them do all the work and pull some double-cross before the gold was divided."

Drew stepped closer to him. "You had better leave here while you can. This meeting is for Tommy's friends, and that doesn't include you."

"I'm a lawyer, Mr. Woodson. I serve the community. I

represent law and order." Smoke escaped Logan's thin lips and billowed in the breeze. "Anyway I liked that young fellow. If he did happen to be dead, I'd wish him back."

Drew's fists clenched.

"Good evening, gentlemen." Benton Farwell, who had been heading to the church door, sidetracked to where they stood. He had done so purposefully, Drew decided, in an attempt to ward off trouble.

"There's some men down at the tavern looking for you," he said to Walt Logan.

Walt Logan, as if glad to leave and maintain face at the same time, tossed aside his cigar and ambled down the street toward the Red Elk. By now the crowd was inside, seated.

Drew gazed through the double doors. He could see the back of Silas' graying hair, the snow-white side-whiskers. He looked very respectable, pious, even. Drew's gaze drifted to his Swedish wife, who still held on to his arm. He wondered if she knew what vengeance Silas was capable of, or if this quality of protecting his own was what made her feel safe in this shot-gun world of Leland.

Silas belonged to this old gold-rush town, but Benton Farwell certainly did not. He should be in some rich city back east. Tonight the tavern owner was dressed with extreme care, light brown trousers, cutaway jacket, and spotless white shirt. Drew glanced at him, then followed the man's gaze to Celene, who had risen and was walking toward the altar.

Once she was standing beside the Reverend, he spoke, "Celene has asked to open this meeting by singing Tommy Garth's favorite song, 'Rock of Ages.'"

Drew couldn't take his eyes from her. Neither could Benton Farwell.

The soft white dress she wore, decorated with lace and tiny seed pearl buttons, looked almost like a wedding gown, except for the wide, pink satin ribbon that decorated the skirt and accentuated her tiny waist. With her cloud of honey-colored hair, she looked just like an angel. And that voice... No wonder Tommy had been so crazy about her.

"Amazing," Benton said, his words an awed whisper. "Celene wants to be a singer more than anything else. And, most certainly, she could succeed."

Drew, his eyes still on Celene, said, "Tommy never mentioned to me that she wanted a career."

"Probably not," Farwell said. "One like that just isn't possible here. I can't ask her to sing in a tavern. She's too good for that. She needs some grand theater."

Drew still watched Celene, but out of the corner of his eye, he noted the open admiration on Farwell's handsome face. No doubt half the men in town were in love with her.

"Did you know, Drew, I used to be an actor," he was saying in his soft, quiet way.

"I don't recall your mentioning it."

"My dream," Benton Farwell said, "has always been to make enough money here to go back east and purchase a theater."

"Let the water and the blood..." Celene's voice suddenly broke and the lines of her song trailed into ghastly silence. She had lost the love of her life, and Drew didn't have to tell her, she knew it. Drew felt her pain, too. He wanted to stride down the aisle, to enclose her in his arms, to stop the sobs that had already begun. He forced himself to remain immobile, to watch in dismay as she, with both hands to her face, stumbled blindly away. The Reverend caught up with her and guided her to a seat.

Farwell and Drew remained standing just inside the doorway during the long prayers. They ended at last with the Reverend's ringing statement, "God in heaven, Father of us all, we implore you to keep your protective arms around our beloved friend, Tommy Garth. Keep him safe, and if you see fit, return him to us. We ask it in Christ's name. Amen."

Feeling choked, Drew stepped to the side of the church as the crowd passed by him. Silas had gone after Celene, but Helga spotted him and came over to stand beside him.

Tears had welled in her eyes, too. Helga loved fiercely and like Silas, protected those she loved. "If you find Tommy," she said, "couldn't you just bury him, never let Celene know!"

"I couldn't do that, Helga," Drew replied. "We all have to face the truth. Celene does, too. But I felt...because of Tommy...that I should talk to her, try to prepare her all I can."

Helga gave his hand an affectionate pat. "Then you do that, talk to her tonight, Drew. Silas and I will leave her with you."

Drew had never felt more ill at ease than he did once Celene and he were alone. He couldn't bring himself to tell her how likely it was that Tommy was dead. He didn't want her to cry again. On the other hand, he couldn't give her false hope. He merely walked beside her toward her home in awkward, stricken silence.

She stopped at the front door. "Helga said you wanted to talk to me."

"Tommy...loved you so much. You know that."

She looked up at him solemnly. He had never seen anyone so beautiful.

"I know. He asked me to marry him. Did he tell you he was going to?"

"Yes. Tommy said he finally had something to offer you. We made a big strike, enough to make us both immensely rich."

"I know. He told me. He told me the minute you found

that vein. He had such high hopes. And they came true." Hit with the irony of her statement, Celene stopped short. The tears he so dreaded appeared again. She made no attempt to wipe them away as they trailed down across her face.

Drew couldn't keep himself from reaching out for her, from pulling her close to him. His hand smoothed her blonde hair, the touch and look of it in the lamp from the window soft and shimmering like spun gold. He tried to comfort her, "Don't cry," he said huskily. "Maybe there's some chance yet. Maybe I'll find him alive."

She shrank away from him. "You know that's not going to happen, Drew. If only things were different. If only I hadn't hurt him. Now I'll always remember how he looked the last time I saw him. How I wish I had said yes! How I wish I had told Tommy I would marry him."

"You didn't tell...but I thought...the two of you..." It seemed impossible for him to put a single ending on any of the sentences. They each trailed off into disbelieving stillness.

"Oh, I loved him, Drew. Like you did. Like a brother. But I just didn't feel about him the way I should have felt. I tried to make Tommy understand. It's not fair for a woman to marry a man she doesn't love in the right way, is it?"

"Are you in love with someone else?"

Celene gazed up at him. That old boldness he had never liked flared again in her eyes. "Yes. But he has never known about it."

Why did Celene keep looking at him so intently? He felt his mouth go dry. He thought of all the times she had visited his home with the Tates. Alluring, charming, Celene had for the past year been close by, laughing, bestowing upon Tommy and him those special smiles. Had Drew been more aware of her than he had ever admitted? Perhaps the real reason he hadn't wanted Tommy to marry her was that he wanted her himself.

* * * *

The next day at dawn Drew and Silas rode out to catch up with the posse. The land before them was dotted with cedars and sagebrush, shadowed by the peaks of distant mountains.

Occasionally Silas would dismount to study fresh tracks left on the bone-dry earth. "They've been this way for sure," he said. "They're probably headed for the high desert county where the sheriff believes Reno hides out."

They crossed a barren wilderness of sand-colored bluffs that looked monotonously the same.

"Let's take a short-cut to the mountains," Drew suggested, "and save some time."

Silas soon drew to an abrupt halt, once more slipping from the saddle and kneeling. "Grooves from a wagon," he said. "Any man without a damned good reason would avoid this rough trail. Reno took it, same as us, to save time."

As they rode on, Drew kept thinking of Joe Dodson, of his long, sun-burnt face, with the narrow, empty eyes, always half-concealed by scraggly beard and dirty-looking sandy hair. He recalled with a tinge of fear the murderous look on Dodson's face when he had drawn on Tommy at the bar.

"Do you think Dodson and Reno stayed together?" Silas asked.

"I hope so," Drew said, "I'd hate to think of what Joe Dodson would do to Tommy if Reno left them alone."

"That Dodson's mean and dumb," Silas replied. "Not a good combination."

Drew spotted the wagon first. It lay on its side at the bottom of a deep ravine where it had probably been pushed. Drew approached the abandoned wagon with apprehension half expecting to find Tommy's body close by.

"Of course it's empty," Silas said, shielding his eyes from

the sun as he looked back. "I reckon they hid the gold before they got this far."

They backtracked a while trying to trace the course of the wagon through the high grass along Ames Creek.

"This is useless," Drew said. "They wouldn't hide the gold anywhere near the wagon anyway. What do you say we go on and find the sheriff?"

"Sure, let's head right for the mountains. If you asked me, there's trouble brewing in Leland. Jeff McQuede might want to get back there in time to stop a lynching."

After a long, hard ride, they spotted a group of men beneath a scattering of aspen. Their approach was met with drawn guns.

"Hold on," the sheriff called. "It's only Tate and Woodson."

The sheriff, burly, with bristly white whiskers, like a four o'clock shadow across his broad jaw, rode forward. "We're on their trail. A while back, we found an abandoned wagon."

"We saw it," Drew said.

"They can't have gotten far," McQuede said, squinting the way he usually did as he indicated the high cliffs that blocked the way. "This is where we're going to split up and make sure no one trapped in that canyon gets by us."

He turned to Silas. "I guessed right. Reno Slade and his gang's sure enough behind this."

"We found Blackjack Logan," Drew told him. "Right now, he's locked in the Leland jail." He explained how they had followed Walt to his hideout.

"There might be trouble. We thought you might want to head back to Leland," Drew said.

"If they get up a lynch mob, so be it," the sheriff replied. "I've been on the trail of Reno Slade for a long time. Everything else be damned, I'm not leaving this canyon until I find him!" He turned to Drew, his tone growing milder. "You boys did some mighty fine work. What else did Logan tell you? Did he know where Slade was headed?"

"No, but if you can believe Blackjack, Joe Dodson's with him. They took Tommy as a hostage. He's hurt pretty bad, if he's still alive."

The sheriff shifted his heavy body in the saddle and fastened his narrowed, level gaze on Drew. "What about the gold?"

"Blackjack knows where they stashed it, but he's not talking," Silas broke in.

The sheriff spat on the ground with contempt, but made no comment.

Jeff McQuede gestured to his men, about a dozen of them, some of them as shady-looking as the bandits they pursued, and they remounted and drew forward. Once they gathered around, he said, "They've holed up somewhere in the canyon, and we're going to find them. We'll split up and ride two together. Once we enter Rabbit Hole Canyon, you four ride with Silas Tate straight through to the other side. You two," he said, "go north, you two, south. The rest of you remain at this entrance. You, Woodson, ride with me."

For a while they rode in silence, searching the area for signs of the bandits, tensely keeping watch on the cliffs above. No wonder Slade and his gang had chosen this area for a hiding place. It was lined with a multitude of caves and shelters where a man could disappear from sight, so many blind ledges and clefts in the rock from where a person could observe unnoticed and get the first shot.

They had reached a crest of high ground when the sheriff stopped abruptly. "What's that? Just below us." McQuede moved ahead cautiously, drawing his gun.

They started down the steep descent. Whoever was at the

bottom of the slope posed no threat. Drew could see only the man's back. He swung from a rope knotted to the thick branch of a cottonwood.

Tommy always favored blue shirts, and this one was dark blue. Drew's chest tightened with dread.

McQuede reached the bottom first, slid from his horse, and stood immobile, looking up in a puzzled way at the dead man's face.

Drew couldn't bring himself to draw closer. He could hear the strained tone of his own voice, not sounding like his, but distant and unfamiliar. "Why did they hang him?" he moaned. "Tommy was badly wounded. Why didn't they just leave him somewhere along the trail to die?"

"You'd better come on down here," McQuede said, "and take a look for yourself."

Drew dismounted and walked down the trail toward the sheriff. His eyes caught first on the hanged man's boots, fancy boots with red-and-black-flanged toes and spurs of etched Mexican silver.

Reno Slade—the fearsome man whose very name struck terror into the hearts of men and women alike, hung, head lolled down, eyes bulging. His heavy, barrel-chested body dragged down the rope until his toes dangled just inches from the ground. His face showed signs of having been bludgeoned.

"Looks like a double cross," the sheriff observed. "Those three bandits must have fallen out over the loot, and this one ends up hanged."

"Joe Dodson was loyal to Slade," Drew said.

"*Was*, that might be the word. Dodson's best friend has always been himself."

Drew stepped closer. "Shall we cut him down?"

"Suit yourself. I sort of like the look of him hanging there."

Drew took out a knife and severed the rope. The beefy man hit the ground hard. Drew turned him over, staring at the bruised and swollen face, at the brown beard matted with blood. Then he noticed the red stains, like stripes across the torn shirt. "He's not only been hanged, but tortured."

"Bet he didn't talk," McQuede said. "Bet he went to his death not breathing a word about where he hid that gold."

Silence stole over them, which McQuede soon broke. "Only two suspects, Blackjack Logan or Joe Dodson. Or maybe both of them working together."

"How long do you think Reno Slade's been dead?"

"Hard to tell. Probably they separated, then when they caught up with Slade again, he refused to share the wealth."

Drew straightened up. It might not have been one of the bandits who had hanged Reno Slade, but the man Silas claimed to have seen lying in wait in the bushes outside his cabin.

He stared at the sheriff. He had always liked Jeff McQuede, put no stock in the rumors that hovered around him. McQuede had a reputation for being too fast on the draw. At the Red Elk Tavern they often talked about how he'd lost his job in Santa Fe for cold-bloodedly gunning down two unarmed men. But Drew always took up for him. He wasn't so sure, though, of some of the members of the sheriff's posse. One or more of them could have found Reno and leapt at the opportunity to hang and torture him, to try to find out for themselves where Reno had hidden the gold.

"Did your posse stay together?" Drew asked.

"No. We covered as wide a territory as possible and met here."

For a long time they stared down at Reno Slade.

"Just another dead outlaw, and a bad one," McQuede said at last, taking a package of tobacco from his shirt pocket. "I guess all's well. This will save the law the trouble of hanging him. Let's go back, Woodson. I'll send some of my men to load him up."

Sheriff McQuede started back up the hill, pausing to glance back at Slade's body. "Logan killed Reno Slade," he said, "with or without Dodson's help." Sheriff McQuede spat a chew of tobacco on the ground. "Blackjack Logan—he's either the devil or the devil's hangman."

* * * *

Drew stopped by his cabin to wash up and change clothes, then he headed into Leland. On the long trail that wound downward into town, he thought about what he would say to Celene. Even though she had declined Tommy's offer of marriage, Drew still believed that she did care very much about him. It would be best to tell her outright that Reno Slade had been Tommy's one and only hope and inform her in no uncertain terms just what it meant now that he knew Tommy had fallen into the hands of his bitter enemy, Joe Dodson.

Dusk had fallen, but an oil lamp still burned inside Tate's Mercantile. Drew entered to find Helga seated behind the counter working on credit tabs. He knew at a glance that she was greatly upset, maybe from one of those frequent tiffs between her and Silas. Little else would drive her to the refuge of after-hour's work.

"Is Celene around?"

Helga's eyes shifted uneasily away from his. "No."

"Where is she?"

"You'd best come back tomorrow."

"She surely won't be gone long. It's almost dark. I'll just hang around here and wait a while."

His statement was met by one of Helga's firm don't-cross-me looks. "You just go on about your business, Drew."

Puzzled, Drew crossed to the door where he turned back

to Helga with a questioning gaze.

"No one listens to me," she said, "not Celene, not Silas, not you. You go about doing just what you shouldn't, all of you—despite the trouble in the air."

"The sheriff is back in town," Drew said, knowing how much she respected Jeff McQuede and thinking this would assuage her worry. "He'll be able to handle whatever happens."

"The sheriff came back to Leland, all right, but I saw him heading out to his cabin a while ago. He left that young deputy in charge of that devil, Blackjack Logan. Why on earth would he take a risk like that at a time like this?"

"McQuede has been riding day and night. He must be exhausted." Even as Drew gave the sheriff excuse, he himself thought it a fool mistake, one uncommon for a man so perceptive.

"Silas and you have done enough," Helga declared. "If there's going to be trouble, let some of the others handle it."

So she was expecting a lynching party to form tonight, and was experiencing lack of control over those she wanted to protect most.

"Where's Silas?"

"How would I know?" Helga's frown deepened. Clearly, she feared Silas would join the vigilante party. In addition to that, Helga would want Celene to leave Leland, to go out to her sister's farm where she would be safe, but by the way Helga was acting, Celene must have defied her, too.

Drew stepped out onto the walkway and looked up and down the street. A restless, rowdy mob had already begun to gather around the jail. Their muffled voices, though he couldn't hear what they were saying, eerily broached the space between them. He watched the men's shifting images that looked unreal and grotesque in the growing shadows of evening.

McQuede's deputy, young and inexperienced, must have locked himself up inside the jail. It looked as if he were going to need all the help he could get. Once Drew had reached the outer fringes of the crowd, he saw Celene. She stood in front of the Red Elk Tavern, one hand tight on Benton Farwell's arm.

Drew halted, anger causing the muscles in his jaw to tighten. Was this the real explanation for Helga's defensive attitude? She hadn't wanted Drew to know that Celene had left the store with the owner of the tavern.

Drew stared at them, his eyes smoldering. Celene hadn't even waited to hear about Tommy's fate before allowing that smooth, would-be actor to start squiring her around.

Benton Farwell, in long, dark coat and top hat, lean and handsome, was speaking confidingly to her. Celene responded with big-eyed absorption.

Drew, despite the fact that he had concerns more pressing, cut across the street toward them. "What's going on?"

They both looked startled, as if he had just dropped out of the sky. Celene recovered first. "Haven't you heard, Drew?"

"Heard what?"

Benton Farwell supplied the answer. "Blackjack broke out of jail." Farwell hurried on, almost guiltily, "I looked out the window and saw Celene among those in front of the jail. I thought a mob was forming, so I went over to get her out of harm's way. That's when I heard the news."

"Benton sent a friend of his out to Sheriff McQuede's cabin to tell him," Celene said. "We're waiting now to see what he's going to do."

"I've been keeping a close watch on things," Benton said importantly. His light, dreamy eyes shifted to Celene and glowed at her look of approval. "I went over to the jail earlier to warn the deputy. I wanted him to know I'd be on hand if he needed help. I knew all along we were in for trouble, but I certainly didn't know it was going to take this form."

McQuede and the man Benton Farwell had sent to summon him appeared in a cloud of dust at the edge of town. Drew's apprehension grew as they approached and he could see the deadpan expression on the sheriff's face. It occurred to Drew that McQuede had left purposefully, that for some reason or another he had wanted Blackjack Logan to escape from jail.

Still on horseback, McQuede addressed the crowd. "My deputy and I are riding out tonight. There's not much we can do until daylight, except maybe find out which way he headed."

Drew strode forward. "How did he escape?"

"They tell me he had a gun. No argument." McQuede gestured toward the gangly deputy who had just ventured outside. "Ollie had to open the cell or die."

"How did he manage to get a weapon?"

McQuede squinted down at Drew. "My deputy let that brother of his in to see him."

"To prepare a case for his defense." Walt Logan announced. All eyes turned to Blackjack's brother as he made his slow, dignified way through the crowd.

"He didn't have any weapons before you got there," the deputy spoke up. "You must have sneaked him that gun some way."

"I wouldn't do that," Walt Logan replied evenly.

"You shouldn't have helped him escape, Logan," McQuede said, pausing to spit tobacco juice on the ground. "He'd be a hell of a lot safer here in jail."

Walt Logan remained composed and silent. Everyone

seemed to be thinking the same thoughts concerning him. His semblance of reform was just a hoax; Walt Logan had never stopped working with Blackjack.

"I had nothing to do with this, McQuede," he said at last and turned to leave.

"I'll ride with you," Drew told the sheriff.

"No, Woodson. I'll tell you the same thing I told Silas. I want some fresh hands tomorrow. You boys get some rest. Meet me, first light, at Rabbit Hole Canyon."

* * * *

Rest—Drew already knew that wasn't going to happen. Distraughtly he sank down at his desk and lifted the little revolver he had taken from Blackjack. With its rounded handle and cylinder barrel, it looked the same as it had when Blackjack had drawn it from his boot—ready to kill, deadly.

Blackjack was sure to go straight for the gold. He had, after all, told his brother he knew right where it was stashed. Unless that was just another one of his many misstatements, unless, Blackjack meant, instead, that he knew Reno had hidden the loot and that he knew right where to find Reno.

What else would explain the torture and hanging of Reno? The sheriff was probably right when he'd called Blackjack the devil. Walt Logan, the devil's hangman, must have caught up with Reno and tried to make him tell where he had hidden the take from the robbery. Reno might have gone to his death without saying a word, but he couldn't take that chance. Drew would get a bite to eat, then start out tonight on his own. He had no other choice if he were to beat the Logan brothers to the gold.

He stepped over to the stove where the smell of wood smoke mingled with the scent of stew and boiling coffee. He dipped himself some stew and had started to return to the table, when he caught the faint sound of shuffling brush from outside the cabin.

Quickly, he lifted Blackjack's little Derringer and moved to the door. Standing off to the right, he pushed it open slightly and tensely skimmed the darkness. Who was out there? Blackjack Logan? Heart thudding, he watched alertly. His eye suddenly caught a movement from the nearby bushes. A form like a black shadow crept haltingly, like some wild animal unsure of a destination, toward the cabin.

Drew took careful aim. But just before he pressed the trigger, he saw the man stagger. He lowered the pistol. "Who's there?"

Silence followed his call. Drew ventured another look. The man had fallen to his knees. Some trick, he thought, to lure him out into the open. He waited, but the form did not stir.

"Answer me or I'll shoot," he called.

A muffled voice, so low he could barely make it out, replied weakly, "It's me."

Tommy's voice—for an instant Drew thought this sense of recognition to be only of his own confusion. But if Tommy had fallen out there, wounded, he couldn't afford to delay.

Grasping the gun, he moved cautiously forward until the boyish features, contorted with pain and fear, became clear. He placed the gun in his boot top and knelt beside Tommy. The kid clutched at him, gripping the front of his shirt in a death hold. Drew could barely make out his words.

"I let you down, Drew." The kid's voice broke. His eyes, black holes filled with the shadows of night, must have brimmed with tears. "I didn't want to die, Drew. If I hadn't opened the safe, Dodson would have killed me. I can't tell you how sorry I am. I ruined us by turning the gold over to them."

"I don't care about the gold. There's more out there. And you and I, we'll find it."

Tommy's voice grew fainter. "Just you, Pard. I'm hurt...real bad. I don't think..."

The sudden, jerky way his words stopped alarmed Drew. He stood up, staring down at Tommy, unable to detect the rise and fall of breath. The kid's clothes were covered with blood. Drew couldn't tell where or how many times he had been shot, but no use trying to find out. If Tommy had any chance at staying alive, it hinged on how quickly he could get him to Dr. Avery.

"You're going to be all right, Tommy. I'm going to hitch up the wagon."

Tommy had not heard him. He had either passed out or...

With nervous hands Drew made hasty preparations. A surge of extraordinary strength enabled him to lift Tommy from the ground to the bed of the wagon. He raced back into the cabin, grabbed a blanket from Tommy's cot, and wrapped it around him.

The old wagon, wheels vibrating, lumbered down the steep trail. When he reached Leland, he pulled to a stop in front of Dr. Avery's house, jumped out, and banged on the door.

The old man, his office in front of his home, soon appeared. They carried Tommy inside, the doctor saying over his shoulder. "Don't need you in here. Get on out, now. Coffee's on the stove."

Drew woodenly backed from the room. In the kitchen, warmed by the heat of the pot-bellied stove, Drew poured himself a cup of coffee. Then he sat down at the table and began a long, despairing wait.

* * * *

What seemed like an eternity later, Dr. Avery, thin, balding, wearing his small, gold-rimmed glasses came into the kitchen. Drew stood up.

"Took a bullet in the back," he said. "Just barely missed his spinal cord. Tommy's lost a good deal of blood and has lots of mending to do." The doctor smiled. "But, all in all, I'd say that boy's name ought to be Lucky."

For the first time in hours, Drew felt able to draw a steady breath. "Can I see him?"

"Just for a short time. I gave him a big dose of laudanum for the pain."

Tommy laid very still, his eyes closed. They opened when Drew smoothed a hand across his light, ruffled hair. "We'll be back mining in no time, partner."

"It all happened so fast."

"Not now, Tommy."

"Right after Celene and the Tates left, Slade, Dodson, and Logan just burst into the cabin." His lips pressed together as if it were hard for him to talk. "They loaded the crates on a wagon. Slade started out ahead. It's then we heard the shots."

"Do you have any idea who was doing the shooting?"

"I couldn't see anyone. Joe Dodson whirled back and a bullet got him full in the chest. Blackjack and I tossed him over his horse. I jumped on the appaloosa and tried to get away. That's when I was struck in the back."

"What happened to Dodson?"

Tommy eyes closed again, and he remained silent as if waiting for his strength to return.

"Don't try to talk, Tommy. All this can wait."

With his eyes still shut, he said, "After a while Slade stopped and put him in the wagon. Dodson kept getting worse. We were headed toward Rabbit Hole, but Slade said we couldn't go on, said he didn't think Dodson was going to make it. We headed northeast and holed up in a little clearing in Grotton instead."

Drew thought of the abandoned wagon they had seen near the narrow mouth of Grotton Canyon.

"The ravine is a perfect place to hide, filled with trees and large boulders. While Blackjack and Slade were trying to doctor Dodson, I managed to get away. I set off running along Ames Creek.

"They didn't follow me. Probably because they knew McQuede would soon be hot on their trail. I was bleeding bad. I must have passed out a while. When I came to, I got disoriented and lost my way. I just kept on walking. It took all this time for me to find my way back to our cabin."

"You get some rest now," Drew said.

Blackjack had not lied about the fourth robber hidden in the bushes at the cabin. He may or may not have lied about their splitting up, about Reno Slade taking the gold to hide, while he attempted to throw the posse off the track.

Sheriff McQuede's assessment of a double-cross between the three bandits could still be true; Reno Slade could have wanted all the gold himself, or Blackjack could have decided to take over his share, too. But since Blackjack had not been a target, the hidden gunman must have been his brother and helpmate, Walt Logan. But how was Drew ever going to prove the identity the man who had shot both Tommy and Joe Dodson?

* * * *

Daylight set a dull, clouded brightness across the rugged line of buildings, penetrating the dim stable already filled with the clang of the blacksmith's hammer. Drew, still shaken, hurried toward Tate's Mercantile, anxious now that Tommy had rallied to share the news with Celene.

Celene worked alone in the store, stacking tins of tobacco from basket to shelf. She looked up, her large, blue eyes widening. "Drew, I was just thinking about you." She stopped her busy work and smoothed her hands across her dress, decorated with vines and tiny daisies. She remained gazing at him, concern moving into her eyes. "Is there news?"

"Only good news."

Celene moved closer to him as he spilled out the story. When she swayed a little, happy tears overflowing, it seemed proper that he open his arms and hold her. She clung to him tightly, her body trembling as she cried.

She felt soft as a morning meadow and with the same fragrance. Drew's arms tightened around her.

"Oh, Drew," she said. "I'm so glad about Tommy."

Her speaking Tommy's name caused Drew to reluctantly let her go. "I've got to get back."

"I'll be right down, just as soon as Helga comes in."

Drew left abruptly. As he approached the doctor's office, he came face to face with Walt Logan. Logan looked different today, less confident, in fact, openly worried. "I've just heard the news. How is Tommy Garth?"

"He's alive, no thanks to the Logans."

"Don't be making that accusation plural. I've told you before, I'm on the side of the law now."

"So you say."

"I don't like you either," Walt Logan said slowly, "but that doesn't mean we can't talk like two reasonable men. I know what you want, Woodson, and I'm about to tell you my goal. Blackjack must be brought in unharmed so I can defend him in a court of law."

"You should be talking to Jeff McQuede, not me."

"Blackjack's in more danger from you. And from your so-called partner."

"What do you mean, so called?"

"Wake up, Woodson!" Logan's voice had grown harsh. "Even you should be able to see that Tommy Garth hired my brother, along with Slade and Dodson, to fake this robbery. Those three fools didn't even consider the fact that if Garth didn't want to share the gold with you, he wouldn't want to divide with them, either." Logan's black eyes flashed. They remained fastened on Drew. "Your little pal is lying to you now, and, you, green as a gourd, are believing him."

Walt Logan started around him, but Drew blocked his way. "Where do you think you're going?"

"It's necessary for my brother's defense," Logan replied coldly, "to get a statement from Garth."

"You're not to be anywhere near him," Drew replied, and remained staring him down until at last Logan turned and headed for the saloon.

Drew went back into the doctor's office and addressed Dr. Avery, who had been watching from the window. "We've got to keep him away," he said.

"Don't worry," the doctor replied, "I will be very careful concerning Tommy's guests."

"What are you saying?" Tommy's voice sounded from the adjoining room. "That I can't even have company?"

"Depends on who," Dr. Avery spoke sternly. "You're here for a while, you know. And I make all the rules."

"Here for a while?" Tommy moaned. "For how long?"

"In a few days, ask me again," the doctor returned.

"I'm leaving just as soon as I can," Tommy responded in his old, spirited way. "Just you wait and see."

"He's going to be difficult," Dr. Avery remarked, smiling.

Drew's gaze lifted to the grandfather clock behind the doctor's desk. He'd have to ride hard if he were going to catch up with Sheriff McQuede. Just as Drew started to go back in and say goodbye to Tommy, Celene entered. She glanced at Drew, then looked away quickly. By this time the news that Tommy would make a full recovery must have reached her, then what could possibly be wrong with her?

"Go on in, dear," Dr. Avery said. "Tommy's been asking for you."

Even though Drew knew he should give them time together, he trailed after her. She leaned over Tommy's bed and kissed him lightly on the forehead. She said gently, "I've found out something important, Tommy. When I thought you were dead, I knew just how wrong I had been. I should have said yes when you asked me to marry you."

Drew halted, immobile. Her unexpected words threw him totally off balance, as if some hard blow to the stomach had winded him. He struggled to recover.

"Did you hear the news?" Tommy said, joy breaking over him. "Before long, Leland's going to have the biggest wedding this town has ever seen!"

Drew hadn't wanted his voice to sound so distant. "I'll be the best man."

"Darn right!"

Celene met Drew's gaze, her happiness over Tommy's return seemed tainted by some deep sense of loss.

* * * *

Tucking Blackjack's little silver-etched Derringer in his boot, packing his rifle and extra shells, Drew started out to catch up with Sheriff McQuede.

The endless stretches of cedars and sage, the sand-colored bluffs, brought a resurgence of Drew's wanderlust days when he had roamed the west as a carefree seeker of fortune. That foot-loose nature had never stopped calling to him, although as of late Tommy had become a part of it, tagging along on his journeys like some rollicking pup.

Drew wished Tommy were riding with him now; he longed to be heading out now on some new adventure instead of toward Rabbit Hole Canyon for a showdown with Blackjack

Logan.

At the wagon the bandits had left abandoned, he hesitated. A dying man, a load of treasure, a pursuing posse—the gold couldn't be stowed far from this very spot.

Casting aside his plan to meet the sheriff, Drew backtracked, following Tommy's directions northeast into Grotton Canyon, the place where the outlaws had spent their final night together.

He sat tensely on the saddle, one hand gripping his rifle as he wound through massive slabs of stone, through blind trails where an enemy could be waiting at any turn. He proceeded cautiously, keeping ever in mind that Dodson despite his injuries might still be alive, might have stayed behind at this lost camp to keep watch over the gold.

During the tedious course of his long, uninterrupted ride, his anxiety began to ease and the high, tan ledges started to take on a monotonous similarity. So many gullies, rifts, and chasms, all perfect places to stash away the fortune they had stolen from Tommy and him.

He felt sure Reno Slade hadn't talked, and the gold, safe and secure, lay somewhere close by, yet stumbling upon that exact place would be impossible. In fact, after a passage of time, the bandits themselves would have a hard time finding the precise location again, unless they had left behind some kind of marker. Drew's gaze wandered across forest and rocks for some telltale sign, a knife stuck in bark, a deep niche in a tree, or an odd arrangement of stones.

Drew eased the roan slowly down to level ground, into a copse of spruce and cedar, like the place Tommy had described. There he dismounted and began to explore on foot. In no time he spotted the long-cold ashes of a campfire.

A cool wind rushed through the canyon as Drew stopped and skimmed the area. His gaze lighted on a large mound covered with rocks. When he climbed up to it, he could see that a tree branch had been scraped of bark and driven deep into the earth. Carved on it in large, amateurish letters were the initials, JD. Dodson's pal, Reno Slade, must not have wanted his friend to be buried in an unmarked grave.

Drew stood over the marker in front of heaping sod covered by rocks intended to keep away the animals. Dodson dead, Reno Slade, dead—only one of the three outlaws remained, Blackjack Logan.

Silas had been right calling Logan the devil. Blackjack must have masterminded the plot from the start, planned all along, with the help of his brother, to kill his two partners and take all of the gold for himself.

If so, Drew could identify the unknown gunman hidden at his cabin as Walt Logan. Logan had opened fire hitting Dodson and Tommy. He had intended to kill Reno Slade, too, so he and Blackjack could leave with the wagon full of gold, but during the gun battle, Slade had managed to escape. Not wanting to lose the gold, Blackjack rode after him.

Dodson, perhaps lingering a while, had died from his wounds. Blackjack must have told the truth; the bandits had split up, leaving Slade to bury Dodson and hide the gold. Blackjack was locked up in Leland at the time Slade was hanged. He must have sent his brother Walt out to serve as executioner, to torture Reno Slade in a futile attempt to make him tell where he had stashed the loot.

A ruthless pair! Blackjack, the devil, and Walt Logan, the devil's hangman.

Drew stared down again at the grave, a chill settling over him and with it a resolve to catch them both.

He hadn't realized how much time had passed. Twilight was casting shadows through thick branches. Uncertain of what course to take, Drew headed on toward Rabbit Hole.

He passed the creek where on his last trip he had found the posse gathered, then he pushed on into the ever-darkening canyon. He rode slowly, hampered by the whistling wind, remaining alert for signs of McQuede and his men.

Drew reached the rise of land where the trail sloped sharply downward, the place where the sheriff and he had found Reno Slade hanged. He started down the slope, then halted, sucking in his breath. Below him from the thick branch of the cottonwood, a dark silhouette swayed with the gusts of wind, swinging like a ghost in the shadows.

At first he thought it some strange play of light that made him think Reno Slade's body still hung from that very same limb. But the image remained before his eyes, eyes, he thought, that must be playing some horrible trick on him.

He moved down the trail slowly. Even before he came close enough to see the curly black hair and drooping mustache, he recognized the dead man—Blackjack Logan.

Drew stared at the lifeless form. Finding Blackjack hanged undercut all of his previous theories. The Logans couldn't have been double-crossing Slade and Dodson, for Walt would not have done this to his own brother.

Drew reined his horse up close to Blackjack and cut the rope. The body fell into a crumpled heap. Drew dismounted and knelt over the young outlaw. Dark bruises marred his face. Ugly blade marks, ones that brought an image of Silas' ever-handy knife, made Drew feel half sick. Blackjack, unlike Reno Slade, might well have talked, yet had received no accompanying mercy.

Drew rose slowly, gripped by a wash of sadness, the kind of remorse he always felt over senseless violence. In death Blackjack looked like little more than a boy, as harmless and vulnerable as Tommy. Drew covered the outlaw's face with his saddle blanket and turned away.

Wherever Jeff McQuede was now, Drew needed to find him and tell him about this unexpected turn of events. Unless the sheriff already knew. He usually planned for his posse to divide and search. Chances are by now some of them would have come across Blackjack's body.

Drew didn't ride any deeper into Rabbit Hole, but retraced his trail back to the canyon's mouth, one question repeating itself over and over: with the other two bandits eliminated, then who had hanged Blackjack Logan?

Drew had always defended Jeff McQuede, hadn't believed the accusations of greed and cold-bloodedness that had followed him to Leland. Drew would prefer to think that some of the outraged townsmen had joined the posse and strung Logan up. He might have believed this, had it not been for the evidence of such cruel torture. No renegade members of the sheriff's posse had committed this act in the name of justice. No, whoever had killed Blackjack, had but one goal.

As he rode, images of the last night the outlaws had spent in Grotton Canyon kept replaying for him. He could almost see Reno Slade and Blackjack Logan waiting for Joe Dodson to die, wondering what to do next. Drew began to ride faster. At that moment he felt he knew exactly where the outlaws had hidden the gold.

* * * *

In the moonlight, Drew stood over the grave of Joe Dodson. He hesitated, preparing himself for the task at hand. Silas would call him squeamish, but Drew couldn't help feeling uneasy about disturbing a man's final resting place.

Resolutely he got a small spade from the mining gear he always carried in his saddlebag and started digging away at the recently turned earth. In no time, steel struck against an immoveable object. Drew flinched as he saw that the blade had come into contact with Dodson's boot. A few more spadefuls uncovered the outlaw's legs. He paused to rest a moment and to wipe sweat from his brow. Then he concentrated his efforts beyond the dead man's booted foot.

Suddenly, his spade struck against solid wood—one of the crates taken from his safe. Dodson had been watching over the gold, after all.

The sheriff had been wrong about the death of Reno Slade being some kind of double-cross, or had he? With a sense of shock Tommy leapt to his mind and Walt Logan's poisonous words echoed around him. "Wake up, Woodson! Even you should be able to see that Tommy Garth hired my brother, along with Slade and Dodson, to fake this robbery. Your little pal is lying to you now, and, you, green as a gourd, are believing him."

No, Drew thought. Tommy might be young, impulsive, and at times even foolish, but he wasn't capable of such bloody betrayal.

Drew turned from the grave, gripped by an uneasy sensation that he was no longer alone. Remembering Tommy's declaration that he had no intention of remaining under the doctor's care, Drew half-expected to see the kid emerging from the trees. Possibly he had heard only an animal rustling through leaves. Trying to convince himself he had a bad case of the nerves, Drew remained immobile.

Without warning, a looming shadow materialized from the darkness. He recognized the gruff voice of Sheriff McQuede. "Just you stay put. You make one move, and I'll have to shoot you."

McQuede advanced, standing opposite of him across the open grave. In the moonlight the sheriff looked every bit as rough and menacing as the outlaws it was his job to chase down.

Drew's heart sank. Maybe the stories about McQuede had

been right after all.

The sheriff kept his six-shooter leveled on Drew as he spoke. "I came across where you hanged Blackjack and I tracked you here." He added with a smile that seemed somehow menacing. "You know, Woodson, you're not supposed to take justice into your own hands."

"Blackjack was already dead when I found him."

"Don't pull that one on me," McQuede said, lifting his gun a little. "I'm no saint myself, and in a way what you did to those three served them right, but I signed on to uphold the law. And that's what I intend to do. I'm taking you in."

Or was the sheriff working for himself? McQuede's gaze dropped to one of the partially dug-up cartons. "I see you've found the gold. Ever since we ran across Reno Slade, I knew that it couldn't be all that far away. Clever, wasn't it, for them to bury it with Dodson?" McQuede kicked at the dirt. "Even though I ran across this grave, I didn't give a thought to digging up that no-good's bones."

Drew's eyes locked on his. The day the two of them had found Slade, Drew had been following McQuede's lead. The sheriff could have steered him to that spot intentionally. Earlier he might have left the posse long enough to have tortured and hanged Slade. Moreover, McQuede was conveniently not around when Blackjack had escaped from jail. If the sheriff had planned to catch up with Blackjack and make him talk, that would account for his showing up here now.

Drew was watching McQuede warily when a shot rang out. The sudden explosion caused him to jump back. The sheriff staggered and fell inches from the grave.

Before he could attempt to reach the sheriff's fallen gun or even determine where the ambusher was concealed, Benton Farwell appeared from out of the shield of trees.

"Stop right there."

The owner of the tavern, as sophisticated and gentlemanly as ever, continued striding toward him. Drew could tell by the expression on his face that he had enjoyed gunning down McQuede. Drew wondered why he hadn't simply fired another shot and eliminated him in the process. Was it because he liked to watch a man suffer before he finished him off?

In the waning light Drew could see the long, white hands, the onyx ring carved with the face of a knight. Farwell's pale fingers fastened with deadly grip on his rifle.

Drew, weaponless, knowing any move he made would be his last, watched Farwell glance toward the sheriff, who he had shot in the back, then peer down into the grave.

"I see I got here just in time to get the gold," he spoke quietly.

"I was careful to make sure no one knew about our strike," Drew said. "How did you find out?" He had no sooner asked than realization poured over him, and he added, "Not from Tommy."

Farwell smiled, a little dreamily, the way he had smiled as he had listened to Celene sing at the church, as he had watched her that day across from the jail when Celene had been gripping his arm and gazing admiringly into his eyes.

"In a round-about way, I did hear about your good luck from Tommy. Tommy told Celene, Celene told me. She loves me, you know. The whole plan was her idea. She wanted us to have the gold so we could realize our dreams."

"I hear she's just accepted Tommy's proposal of marriage," Drew responded.

Drew could tell by the way Farwell's lips compressed that Celene had not told him about her new plans. He still didn't believe it, the fact that Celene was cold-hearted to the core. She had sold Tommy out for Farwell and a chance at a singing career. When Farwell had failed to find the gold, she had switched her affection back to Tommy, believing that Tommy had thrown in with the bandits and had ended up with the entire strike himself.

Not that Benton Farwell couldn't match her for treachery.

"At your saloon, you must have overheard the bandits planning to attack my cabin. You hid out there to ambush them and take the gold."

"Not very successful," Farwell said, "but I tried."

"Instead of joining the posse, you went off on your own." Drew's words conjured up pictures of Farwell hiding as he had just done, taking Reno Slade by surprise. "But no matter what you did to him, Slade wouldn't talk, would he?"

A cruel light lit his eyes, made them large and bright as if he were looking out over an audience from some make-believe stage. "I had better luck with Logan."

It hadn't been kindness of heart that had prompted Farwell to help keep the mob from lynching Blackjack. He had his own plans for the young bandit. He, not Walt Logan, had gone into the sheriff's office and slipped the weapon to Blackjack so he could escape. More cruel and devious than the worst of the outlaw gang, Farwell had double-dealt Blackjack, too. He had promised to aid him, but had waylaid and hanged him instead. But not before he had tortured him into revealing what Reno Slade had not—where the gold was hidden.

Drew glanced toward the sheriff, anxious for some sign of life, but seeing only his broad back and the ever-widening circle of blood that soaked through his shirt.

McQuede's forty-four had slipped from his hand and lay on the edge of the grave. Drew judged he had no chance at all of reaching either it or his own rifle still attached to his saddle. He could feel the pressure of Blackjack's small gun at the top of his boot. But he would be dead before he could pull it free.

Drew stared at Farwell. The saloonkeeper, despite his fine clothing, his fair hair, and chiseled features, was as dangerous a man as he had ever faced. His lust for wealth and for winning Celene had given him the courage to take on three formidable bandits—and win. Benton Farwell might not be the devil; that role belonged to Celene herself, in the guise of an angel. Farwell was merely Celene's tool—the devil's hangman.

As if Farwell could read his thoughts, he said, "A woman like her can drive a man half-crazy," Farwell went on in that quiet voice of his. "I'll get the gold and leave you two out here, dead. No one will ever suspect me. And then Celene and I will have our theater! She will awe the audiences with her marvelous singing." His voice rose theatrically. "And I will play the staring role!"

What a man like Farwell couldn't resist was drama. If that was what he wanted, Drew would supply it. "You don't have to kill me, Farwell." He raised his arms imploringly, hands quaking with fear. "You can have the gold, all of it! I swear I won't tell anyone." Drew's words broke with a sob. "Please, please don't kill me. I'll do anything if you let me live!"

Pretending to be in a state of total collapse, Drew swayed, as if he were going to drop to his knees to beg for mercy. As Drew bent over, his hand closed over Blackjack's gun. The shaking, the pleading, had stopped, had changed into cold resolve as he drew and fired.

Farwell, seeing too late what Drew was doing, pressed the trigger of his rifle, but Drew ducked to the side. The bullet zinged inches from his head. Farwell dropped his gun and grasped his stomach, fingers filling with gushing blood. He reeled backward, eyes widening in stunned surprise, before he fell.

Drew examined him. Farwell was badly hurt, but the shot

had not killed him. With dread Drew moved over to the sheriff. He knelt beside McQuede, gently turning him over.

His face, dead white, blended with the snowy stubble of beard. His features managed to look rough even though wan and still. Drew leaned closer hoping to detect some faint rise and fall of breath. "McQuede."

As if in response to Drew's call, McQuede's eyes flickered open.

"Lie still. You've lost a lot of blood,"

"I...heard...everything."

"Don't try to talk," Drew said with concern. "There's nothing I can do for you here. I'm loading you two up and taking you back to town."

"Cover up the gold first," McQuede gasped. "I'll send my deputy back after it."

* * * *

Drew saw Celene only once more. Jeff McQuede, who had refused to stay in bed despite his wound, was escorting her off to jail. Celene, eyes bold and filled with hatred, stopped to look at Drew, but she did not speak.

Silas stood by and watched, rugged features hard and set—maybe he had already seen it all, maybe nothing existed in this land Silas couldn't take in stride. Helga was sobbing as if her heart would break, but Drew felt confidant Silas would see her through this tragedy.

On the way to fill Tommy in on the news, Drew stopped by Walt Logan's law office. "I'm sorry about Blackjack," he said with sincerity.

A flash of pain broke through the stoniness of Walt Logan's eyes. "Thanks. I didn't expect to hear that from you. Or from anyone."

"He was just a kid, one that in time you might have been able to straighten out."

"I always thought so, but deep inside I guess I knew it wasn't going to happen. I've spent these last few years trying to stop him from making the same mistakes I made when I was his age." Logan rose slowly to his feet. "He got in too deep with Reno Slade and his gang to ever get out."

"He'd want you to have this." Drew took out Blackjack's silver-etched Derringer and placed it on the desk. "Blackjack's gun saved my life. If I hadn't been carrying it, I would be a dead man."

* * * *

As Drew walked toward the doctor's house, he thought about how to break the news about Celene's arrest to Tommy. Drew found Tommy sitting up in bed, long legs dangling over the side, looking none the worse for his close brush with death.

"This time, I turned her down," Tommy announced before Drew could say a word. "Can you believe that? What a fool I am! The most beautiful woman in town wants to marry me, and I turned her down!"

"What are you talking about?"

"Celene. The wedding. I called it all off." Tommy didn't seem in the least disappointed. "She came to visit me and things just didn't seem right. She asked more questions about the gold than she did about me or about our future together. It was all pretend with her, Drew, and all of a sudden I realized it. She never cared about me at all."

"You're right about that." Drew told Tommy about Celene's involvement with Farwell and about how the two had planned the robbery together. After a while, he said, "There'll be another girl for you, Tommy, the right one. And when you find her, you'll know, just like I did with Ella."

"You still miss her, don't you?"

"Always will." Drew remained silent for a while. "The

sheriff had our gold transferred to a jail cell and guarded it. Suppose McQuede deserves a little reward for that. A while ago the stage picked it up, so it's on its way to a bank vault in Colorado Springs. Half yours, half mine." Drew smiled. "Now you can live that good life you talked about in Denver."

"That gold—it hasn't brought us anything but trouble so far. Still, I won't argue, it's nice to have a little back up in the bank. We'll never have to worry about grubbing out a living again." Tommy fell silent, looking a little unhappy. "I don't know if I really want to spend the rest of my life smoking cigars and playing cards."

"Never did sound like anything I'd fancy."

"Then what are your plans, Drew? You going to move to Denver?"

Drew shook his head. "Not me. I just don't fit in with the city life. No, I reckon pretty soon I'll be heading out for Yukon Territory. Who knows? I might get lucky again and hit another strike."

"In that case," Tommy replied eagerly, his face lighting with one of those boyish grins, "I think I might just tag along."

ABOUT THE AUTHORS

L. Jackson and V. Britton are a co-authoring team who have published over thirty novels. Their works have been produced in paper, audio and electronic format. Jackson is from central Kansas and Britton is from Wyoming.

For your reading pleasure, we welcome you to visit our web bookstore

WHISKEY CREEK PRESS

www.whiskeycreekpress.com